Dead End Thrills

By: G. K. Keaton

ARTOFFICIVL.COM

Book design by Gabriel K. Keaton
Map by Gabriel K. Keaton

ISBN: 978-1-6972-1049-1
Imprint: Independently published

www.artofficivl.com

For My Bear

Life is a story. History, her-story, it all has a beginning and middle. And even if we don't know when it's coming, it has an end.

With that said, I think we forget that at some point, we will be a main character in someone else's story, too. We will play a role in somebody else's movie, help turn the page in someone else's book, be the reason for the emotion hitting so hard in a stanza of a poem.

No matter what metaphor you use, it's true. You just can't help it. You can't control the genre, the narrative, and you probably won't be able to see the final product. You won't even know the impact you will have in most people's stories or the impact their story will have on you. It's just something we can't control.

I'll go as far to say we don't even control our own stories. Okay, maybe we do, but not entirely. We are constantly living out the choices, guesses, and mistakes of a dumber and younger us. Whether that version of us be six months younger, two years ago, or an hour beforehand, every choice we made is by someone who simply lacked whatever information we have now that we didn't have before. Most of the time, things turn out great. Sometimes there's that one thing that happens that pops up and makes us feel like our whole life is derailed. When that happens, we harp on it and dwell on it and relive it, but for what? If I would've known I was going to lose my wallet if I went to that bar, I would have stayed home. If I had known that was raisins instead of chocolate chips, I wouldn't have taken a giant bite of that cookie.

Some mistakes I've learned from, like falling in love. I won't do that one again. Regardless of how you think that sounds, I know I'm writing my story the right way. I'm not choosing some unknown adventure of a relationship just so I can end up with a broken heart.

Heartbreak wouldn't be so bad if you didn't do it alone, but you do. Drunk karaoke nights to sad songs, paper cuts on old love letters you kept, eating ice cream on the toilet because you are lactose intolerant, but you're sad so you hope to maybe shit your heart out… No, thanks. I think because I tried to be so in control of my story, I lost control. Not because of the "younger me" analogy—I have been on the same page with myself for quite some time. At some point, I ended up in one of those roles in somebody else's story. New friends become close friends, then plot twists drove me right back to a Dead End and heartbroken.

All you are is just another character in a show, an extra in a movie, a twist in a plot while following the actions of a younger, dumber, unsuspecting version of yourself until your finale. Could be that the chapter ends and you're left behind because you missed your cue to forward the story. All love stories end in tragedy if you wait long enough, but for you, you'll be killed off in the first ten minutes of a romance movie you didn't know you were in.

Maybe you added one extra syllable to that haiku, and now you've ruined everything. You walk out on stage and take a bow, anticipating boos, praying for applause, but getting what from your performance?

Will the journey down this road all be worth it?

CHAPTER ONE
(201mi)

"*The small round of applause snapped Caleb out of his daydream. He joined in, not knowing or caring what the celebration was for. Caleb was distracted and clearly had other things on his mind.*"

The clapping came quickly to an awkward halt as people looked around to see where the weird narration was coming from.

"People, please. Let's try to ignore that voice, and maybe he will go away. Now, would anybody else like to share with us today?" the group leader pleaded, trying to hide his annoyance.

"I mean, like who is that?" a woman said, looking behind her to the bleachers.

"Ma'am, please. I assure you it's nothing. Again, any sharers?"

"*Caleb was annoyed. Sure, his personal demons that had been plaguing him to break down or even seek help were annoying, but could it also be this cult's leader? Was it the way he was dressed, in his red t-shirt*

5

that *was* tucked into his cargo shorts, or his overly concerned tone in everything he said? Something about the man definitely annoyed Caleb. 'He's honestly probably a nice guy,' Caleb thought to himself."

"Excuse me!" The group leader directed his voice a few feet away, to a dark corner on the bleachers. He was sure that's where the voice was echoing from, but again was met with an uncomfortable silence.

"*The voice lowered his, um, voice and persisted with his story. The group leader gained the attention of everyone in his little chair circle, but only for a moment. The doors of the dimly lit gym opened and closed in the distance, followed by bickering whispers. It was Caleb's friends trying to figure out how to extract him from his current situation without disrupting the—unbeknownst to them—already disrupted meeting. A heavyset man broke the circle of awkward silence and stood up, causing his chair to squeak a sigh of relief.*"

"Sir, could you please not!"
"That's quite alright," the nervous man said to the group leader. He nervously twisted his camouflage baseball cap in his hand while avoiding eye contact with anyone. "I'd like to share something if

y'all don't mind," he continued in a shaky, deep southern tone.

"Thank you, Jerry," the group leader welcomed. "Your courage is very much appreciated here. Please share."

"Caleb stumbled out from the shadows, now speaking in full narrator volume. He concluded that not only was it the cult leader's tone that annoyed him, but also the fact he was bursting at the seams with problems he wanted to get off his chest. Caleb interrupted Jerry before he could speak again."

"Actually, I have something I want to share abo-"
"Yeah, but—"
"Don't be courageous now, Jerry. I got this," I retorted.

Jerry looked up from the floor to the group for some sort ⌐king, but was met with a consen⌐ ion. The group leader ⌐ ⌐ing deeply, ⌐⌐ ⌐c was left of his

"As Jerry sat down, Caleb put his hand on Jerry's sticky, sweaty shoulder to help him balance himself while he stood swaying back and forth."

7

"Hello, my name is Caleb and I have a problem."

"Unfortunately, we all know who you are. You've been narrating it to us for the past fifteen minutes," the leader said through his teeth, trying to force a smile.

"Well, yeah, I'm telling a story."

"Caleb. Have you been drinking?"

"-the man asked me with heartache, his voice now sending my arm hair straight up with annoyance-"

"Would you cut the shit!" the group leader demanded.

"Yeah, I am. So what if I'm drunk? That's not why I'm here. That's not my problem!"

"I think it is your problem," Jerry mumbled under his breath.

"Hey, screw you, Jerry!" Before I could finish, my friends rushed over to me and proceeded to drag me out in the middle of my ramblings. "My problem is with Brooklyn!"

THIS night is when I knew I had hit sort of a rock bottom. I haven't narrated like this since my parents' divorce; and usually I only do when I'm feeling, well, what I felt tonight. The story doesn't start here, but it's the perfect place to start telling it.

8

"Sorry, guys. He doesn't need to be here, but keep fighting the good fight," Joelle said while hoisting me up on his shoulder.

"Excuse me, what is the meaning of all of this?" the group leader demanded.

"Hey, shut up, Jerry!" AJ screamed out while holding me up on the other side.

"Dude, that's not Jerry," I belched out to him.

"Yeah, I am," Jerry responded.

"Anyone ever tell you that you're a know-it-all, Jerry?" AJ yelled out before he and Joelle dragged me through the gym door. They stuffed me in the back of Joelle's two-door Subaru and we sped off as if we were suddenly in a drag race.

"Aw, man, slow down. My head's spinning," I moaned.

"Dude, we haven't even moved yet. He just put the car in reverse, foot still on the brake," AJ heckled.

"All-time low man, drunk at an AA meeting?" Joelle lectured before pulling off.

"Maybe if you spent more time with me and Caleb on PS4…" AJ mumbled under his breath.

"Really? Is now really the time?"

"Guys," I interrupted.

"We'll finish this later," AJ said to Joelle. "Yeah, buddy, what's up?" He turned around on his knees, planting them in the seat to look at me.

"Come on man, seatbelt," Joelle
bickered. He was met with a middle finger
pushed into the side of his cheek.

"I am here for you, Bud," AJ said to
me.

"Can you guys just drive me
somewhere?" I asked.

"Anywhere man, you name it."

"Dude. Do you have gas money?" Joelle
tried to whisper to him, and was again met
with a middle finger.

"Take me back to Brooklyn."

They got quiet, and AJ turned around
in his seat. We sat silently for a moment,
listening to the car engine hum as Joelle
shifted gears.

"How about you crash at my place
tonight. You need the sleep," Joelle
offered.

I didn't answer. I just stared out the
window.

I wasn't always like this. Well, maybe
I am on occasion, but this week,
particularly this past Tuesday, the façade
I'd built up since moving here has slowly
melted away. It's funny when people
describe me; it's always a list I can't
completely agree with.

Charming
Popular
Outgoing
Funny

10

Honest

Easy to talk to

That's the "me" people tell me I am. A version of me I've either subconsciously projected to them, or a version people have unfairly painted me to be. When it comes to me being *charming*, debatable. I'm not *popular*. Maybe by association, since AJ is the sports star of almost everything on campus, and he was the first person to actually befriend me. The mirage of me being *outgoing* has to be the most amusing to me. Mainly because if I am out, it's because I am forced to be wherever the out is. Joelle and AJ are often dragging me places, but the social introvert in me manages to survive with little to no casualties. The word *funny* I'd rather exchange for sarcastic, and if you add the words 'sometimes brutally' in front of the word *honest*, then sure, we can leave them on the list.

To give myself the benefit of the doubt, I am pretty easy to talk to. I love hearing people's problems and silently comparing them to my own to remind myself that people are way more fucked up than I am. I'm not like that with Joelle and AJ though; they are just great to be around. I listen to them fight like a married couple because it's funny. I'm usually instigating and mediating for whatever side I can benefit from the most laughs in the moment,

11

but not today.

　　More often than not, I enjoy a good melancholy mood: a nice rainy day, a Spotify radio station curated off of Simon and Garfunkel, black and white French movies from the 1960s, the sad episodes of *Dawson's Creek* and *The O.C.* I have queued up on my Fire Stick—only the sad episodes. But this mood here lately is more than just melancholy. I don't want to be dramatic and call it depression, but I think a case could be made.

(194 Miles to Destination)

CHAPTER TWO

(2247mi)

I have an addiction. Not of alcohol or
drugs or something interesting like
gambling. I'm more of an addict for new
things, I guess. I have an addictive
personality. I'm not sure if that's the
clinical term—there may not even be one—but
if I am introduced to something new, boy,
look out.

One year, I tried juicing for the
first time, and three months later I was at
PETA rallies, encouraging a vegan
lifestyle. I was kicked out when they
caught me at a popular fast food place
ordering a ten-pack of nuggets for $1.49.
Who could pass up a deal like that? It's a
steal. I mean, let's be honest, most people
aren't even sure that their meat is
actually even meat, so technically I had an
argument to make.

One summer, I went to meetings. I met
alcoholics, gamblers, shoppers and
smartphone junkies. I followed the twelve-
step programs—most of them, anyway.
Needless to say, I was kicked out for

quote-unquote 'not needing help,' which I think is a relative term.

Something one of the group leaders said to me that summer stuck with me: *You are extorting real-life issues for attention because you were raised without being hugged enough as a child.*

Honestly, I think I was probably addicted to being around people who were also addicted to things. Which in hindsight could have gone way more left than it did.

But this isn't a story about addiction. I'm not even sure if you can call it a love story. But it is a story about love.

I felt like it would do me some good to get out of the "big city" of New Jersey. The decision came after a week of hell, about two weeks ago.

I lost my job on a Monday. That Wednesday, a girl I had been seeing for a little over a year got engaged to her boyfriend. Then, on Friday, my grandma left a voicemail on my mother's phone saying she was sick.

Grams purposely made her message vague because she knows my mother is a worrywart. Grams knew that just saying she was sick would make my mom think she had anything from a common cold to the Ebola virus—and choose the latter. So me being the selfless person that I am, I saw an out to get away from the crumbling everyday routine that was my life. I left to take care of my grandma.

As an added consolation, it gave me a chance to get away from my parents, who had recently split. I was able to mask my escape from them when I found out the college down there was starting classes soon. My mom had started bugging me about school, since she didn't have my dad to get on about anything anymore.

Looking back, it felt like a long time coming. They were just 'trying some things differently' was how they explained it to me. Dad slept on the couch many nights. They would have arguments about hair left in the shower. They would fight about making a list before going to the grocery store.

When I was about fifteen, they had this charade where there would be some drag-out fight about something I would only catch the tail end of. Then my dad would move to a new place, so they could give each other space. Then, a month or so later, we would move in with him. This went on for a few years before they realized it wasn't working.

They would take turns disappearing for nights at a time after arguments. When my dad left, my mom would be up crying till early in the morning. The next day, she would pretend like she was fine.

When mom left, my dad would be a wreck day or night. He'd play sad records while explaining what the lyrics meant to him and take pills to help him sleep.

When they did come together, it was with empty apologies and using me as a scapegoat to continue their relationship. That's why I'd have to say there may have been some accuracy to the whole 'not being hugged enough as a child' thing that group leader told me.

If this was love, I didn't want any part of it. Who would want to be a part of a constant game of will-they-or-won't-they? I had seen the mental toll it took on my mother and my dad's dependence on pills because of their relationship.

What confused me the most about it all is that they weren't bad people. They were just bad together, I guess. When they told me about the divorce, I cried tears of joy, though it still hurt to see the inevitable. I guess a part of me was still rooting for them, too, you know? I imagined at the wedding when they had repeated the vows of 'for better or for worse' before God and all of their close friends, they had meant it.

It wouldn't be the first or last time I was wrong about something.

Because no one in my house ever talked about their feelings, or really cared to ask me how I felt about all of this, I turned to the TV. I knew exactly how Dawson Leery felt when the same thing happened to his parents, I was just less dramatic.

Love is merely a fairytale. Another false concept fed to children in cute little animated characters. One day it's a smooth ride into the sunset and then, BAM! The emergency brake is pulled and there's an immediate stop at the 'Happily Never After Station.'

Ironically, that's why I'm on a train now, to get away from everything. Venturing far, far away into the unknown—or the south, as the rest of the world called it. It's been a little over a week, and my grandma had refused to give more detail about the cryptic voicemail. She also refuses to go into a home, so I am going to be taking care of her.

Leaving Jersey for the first time isn't really so stressful if I compare it to a movie. Not one like *The Blair Witch Project,* where I get talked into going in the woods, getting lost, and then losing my life. More of an adventure where maybe I get powers or something, like Michael B. Jordan did in that movie *Chronicles.*

"Hey, kid," the conductor, or whatever his train title was, said to me, interrupting me from the daydream I was lost in. "We are about ten minutes away from your stop."

"Thank you," I said with a lump in my

17

throat. I felt like a jerk for dismissing
his title after he remembered my concerned
inquiry about missing my stop six hours
ago. I've always been sensitive about my
age because I look younger, a trait I was
blessed with from my mom. That same
blessing doubles as a curse with my
inability to grow any facial hair as a
grown-ass man. The man didn't mean any
harm. He could be the conductor, for all I
know, and had left the train on autopilot
to rescue me from any potential lingering
anxiety attacks.

I grabbed my bags from the overhead
compartment, then looked at my watch.
12:45pm. I contemplated if I should go
straight to the campus or to my grandma's,
since the day was about over. Then I heard
her voice ringing in my ear, *Better late
than never,* like some sort of senile
subconscious.

The train crawled into the station,
and I was the only person to get off. I
tried to think what sort of symbolism or
foreshadowing that could have meant, but I
didn't like any of the conclusions.

The air here was different, I thought.
Fresh, maybe? I even thought the sun burned
a bit brighter. Maybe without all the
toxins in the air filtering out the sun's
rays I'll be able to deepen the melanin in
my beige khaki skin. I walked around the
side of the building through the tall, wet

grass while bugs hissed, chirped, and stalked me until I got back to the sidewalk.

The place reminded me of a short I had submitted about a haunted train station in the middle of nowhere. I wished I could have had this experience before I sent it off. Not my best work, but I'm a decent storyteller if you can follow nonlinear points of past, present, and future. It sounds chaotic, but there is a science to my madness, and it's easier to follow if it's already been written down.

When I came to the street side of the train station, I saw a man in what appeared to be a taxi passed out in his driver seat. The car was a poorly painted yellow pinto. Each tire had a different hubcap, and there was no driver side mirror. The driver lay comatose with his face covered by a black baseball cap.

"Hey, man. Are you working?" I asked.

"Does it look like I'm working?" the guy replied, muffled through his hat. I knocked on the window right next to his head, and he snatched his hat off his face and got ready to cuss me—until he saw the wad of money in his face.

"Well, good morning, boss!" he said while unlocking the doors. I gave the driver the address and watched him type it into the TomTom GPS suction-cupped to his windshield. I didn't know if I was more

19

shocked that he didn't have a smartphone or
that the TomTom still worked.

He started up the car and mumbled
under his breath about how he couldn't
believe this town was two hours away, and
then we were on our way.

It was weird watching all the trees
fly by outside the window, clustered
together like they were trying to keep warm
since losing leaves in the cooler weather
approaching. I tried to force nostalgia to
kick in and imagined a mental movie reel
where I would watch memories of me here, as
a child, but it didn't work. The reality
was I had only been down once, when my
grandma moved from Jersey back to her
hometown. Still, the rolling hills of cow
pastures and hay bale graveyards were
soothing. The scenery charmed me, and I
felt that nap I had fought on the train
slowly rush over me.

I blinked, and before I knew it, the
cab driver was tapping me on my knee.

"Come on, man, let me sleep," I
moaned.

"This here is your town," he said.

I looked up. We were driving past an
old supermarket that looked like it hadn't
been used in a decade. Across the street
was a series of small churches, all
different denominations. A gas station
named something Grocery punctuated the end
of the street. I saw a group of houses of

different sizes and shapes that looked like they all shared a front yard ornamented by children's toys. Going around a bend, we waited at one of the only two traffic lights in town. I could feel the walls of the small town closing in on me as I second-guessed my decision.

This must have been how Dorothy felt; I was definitely not in the city anymore.

I looked at my watch. 1:30pm. I wanted to go straight to Gram's place, but she would have killed me for missing the entire day. I let him drive pass Gram's street and continue on.

"Hey man, you mind making a left here at this parking lot?" I asked as we passed the local watering hole—a grocery store.

"To this high school?"

"It's not a high school. It's a university."

"Is this one of the annex buildings?"

"Nope, this is it. This is the campus."

"Small university," he added while pulling into a parking space. I was slightly annoyed. He could clearly read the gold lettering on the side of the building that said Theodore Twombly Community College, but I bit my tongue.

"What about your luggage?" he continued. I ignored him. I had everything I owned with me, smothering in the back seat of his sweaty car, how could I forget.

I grabbed my stuff and threw twenty dollars' worth of ~~bills~~ up front.

"Keep the change!" I yelled as I fumbled towards the doors.

"Aye man, this isn't thirty-five!" he cried out.

I ignored him and walked through the doors of the main building. People were pouring out into the hallway in the distance. I walked slowly, trying not to look awkward with two duffle bags and a rolling luggage. Along the walls were pictures of past sports teams on one side and trophies, ribbons, and memorabilia on the other. As I passed the gym, I saw some guys playing basketball and instantly began to envy the strangers.

I could smell food in the lounge, and my stomach growled at the thought of not eating since lunch yesterday. I finally found the registrar on the right, encased in glass. I walked through the door and stood at the counter for what felt like forever before anyone acknowledged I was there.

"Hi, how can I help you?" the older lady at the counter asked with the biggest smile.

"Today is my first day and I forgot my login to get my schedule."

"Well, welcome!" she said excitedly. The southern twang in her voice made me believe I truly was welcomed. "What is your name so I can print your schedule?"

"Caleb Stevens," I unenthusiastically answered. She fumbled through some papers for my lackluster name. Maybe now that no one knows me I can change my name or go by something different. Something cooler. I should make a new name to match my new path—a stage name, even. Maybe an alter ego of sorts, living up to my grandmother's expectations of me.

Caught up in designing my new alias, I barely noticed a girl had been saying 'excuse me' to get around me. She brushed me to the side to hand some papers to another one of the ladies behind the counter. I only caught a glimpse of her as she turned to leave the office, but I swear I heard Jay-Z's "Excuse Me Miss" play in my head. The smell of honey and lavender lingered after she passed me.

I had never seen this woman in my life, but I felt like I had known her every second of it. Now I was intrigued, because I wasn't easily impressionable. At least that's what I told myself.

I turned back to the counter and saw the woman waiting patiently to hand me my folder. Her super-southern charm outshined her dwindling patience for my daydreaming.

"Thank you, ma'am. I hope everyone here in this town is as kind as you are."

"Well, bless your heart, Cal," she said in a tone as sweet as iced tea. She

23

almost made me forget the fact that I hated when people shortened my name without permission, but it still stung all the same. I bit my lip so I wouldn't correct her and turned to leave when I saw my pile of luggage on the chair by the door.

"Um, excuse me Mrs.…" I waited for her to fill in the blank, remembering I had never asked her name.

"White. Elizabeth White," she replied, smiling. I laughed for a moment, thinking she was joking, but she didn't seem to have a follow up punchline.

"Your name is Betty White?"

"No," she said, losing all expression in her face, "Mrs. White."

"Oh, okay, sorry. Umm, do you mind if I leave my luggage here until the end of the day? I didn't have time to go home before I came-"

"Yes. Yes I do mind. Take it with you. I will not be responsible for your belongings." She stormed away from the front counter and over to a desk in the back. I felt like the only friendship I'd made so far, I had ruined just that quick. Walking down the hall, I couldn't help but dwell on the fact I hadn't corrected her on calling me Cal. I mean, Betty White is a cool name. She should feel flattered; she's a Golden Girl, for crying out loud.

I tried to decipher Betty's handwriting for my schedule. The two rooms

I walked by on my right were math classes, which I was fortunate enough to not have to take. I ignored my instinct to make a left, and instead I continued down the long hall in front of me. Deciding that the room number for my last class of the day said 'four, zero, nine' and not 'nine, at sign, backwards b' my search had come to an end. I took off the duffle bags and sat everything to the side of the door and knocked.

I was waved in and met by fifteen pairs of staring eyes. I tried to ignore them.

"Hi. I'm looking for Literary Arts 102."

"Why?" the short old man asked. He was clearly annoyed that I had interrupted his lesson.

"I'm new here and this is my last class today."

"You are late, Mr.…" He waited for me to say my name. I hadn't had any time to think of an alias yet.

"Stevens, sir."

"Alright, Mr. Stevens sir." The room giggled at his poor attempt at a joke. Or maybe that was the actual funny part. "Take a seat."

"Thank you." I took a deep breath, turned around and grabbed all my bags, and dragged them in with me. The room giggled again, louder this time, at the sight of me fumbling towards the back of the room.

"I came straight from the train station here," I volunteered an explanation, "so I didn't have time to take my stuff home. I really didn't mean to be late."

"It can't be helped now. Take your seat quietly, please."

I slowly piled my stuff in the back of the room, then made my way to the only empty seat in the class. It was in the middle of the rest of the students, and I had to squeeze past several of them to get there.

"As I was saying," the professor said impatiently before I could get to my desk. Sitting in the uneven-legged desk, I noticed everyone following along from a textbook, which I hadn't had a chance to buy yet, and taking notes. It was then I remembered I'd left my laptop bag in the back seat of the taxi I shortchanged.

I slumped down in my desk to sulk when an open book landed in front of me. I looked over to see who the book belonged to, and it was the girl from earlier in the office. She lifted her desk slightly and inched closer to me, then motioned for me to scoot back towards her.

Nervously, I dragged the desk, sending a shriek through the room. I stared at the pages as if I couldn't feel the professor giving me a death stare. He continued his lecture, which coincidently turned into why you should value other people's time and which dissociative disorders you could have if you don't.

In the midst of that was when my life changed. On August 14th, that girl spoke three words that I would never forget.

Hi, I'm Brooklyn.

CHAPTER THREE

After class I had to stay behind to talk to Dr. Paul about everything I had missed, which wasn't much because the first 45 minutes was just introductory. He monologued on about how rude it was to disrupt his class and that sometimes late isn't always better than never, like some sort of bitter villain. My brain wandered in the midst of him talking as my ears muffled his voice with the echo of that girl's introduction.

Brooklyn.

I was pissed I didn't get a chance to thank her properly for sharing the book with me. Chivalrous, I know.

The cues of him wrapping up his ramblings drew me back into the conversation as he ended with … *don't make the same mistakes I made as a kid, and stop being an asshole.* Oddly enough, that was a phrase I've heard all too many times.

Stop being an asshole.

I collected my bags, filled with my

life, from the back of the room and walked down the hallway. I walked around campus and introduced myself to all my professors.

When I went to speak to my art teacher, there was a student sleeping in a desk. She motioned me to be quiet and tip-toe in. She told me that she had let him sleep through the end of class so he would miss his bus for the away game. She also added that I would get the same tough love treatment, if not tougher, because she saw 'my potential' in my portfolio I had submitted in my transfer. I felt like that's something she told every student she met with, but it fueled my ego all the same.

When I was leaving, I purposely dropped the handle to my rolling luggage in front of the sleeping guy's desk. He sat up quick and looked at the clock on the wall.

"Damn it, Valspar, you let me sleep?" he complained.

"Do you want to be written up for your language, AJ?"

"This isn't high school anymore, damn it." I left the room but could still hear them going back and forth.

I turned the corner to walk to the exit, and there she was in the distance.

Brooklyn.

I started an awkward jog, as fast as I could with my bags weighing me down. She pushed the door open and stopped in the doorway to tie her shoe. I slowed down to catch my breath, or maybe it was my nerves. I thought about yelling out to her, but she finished with her shoe and walked into the light.

This is where AJ and I became friends. I'm 5'10", so he had to be at least 6'3". White guy. Besides him being in a football uniform, he was an obvious jock. He was stocky and looked like he had been working out since third grade, with dark curly hair peeking out from under a camouflaged Yankee cap. He walked up to me while I was gasping for air and put his hand on my back. People in the south are friendlier than I was prepared for, but I was too exhausted to shake him loose.

"Thanks for waking me back there, man," he said in a surprisingly less country accent than anticipated.

"Yeah man, no problem."

"She thought I was going to miss my bus, but the game was postponed. I'm AJ." I straightened up from my exhausted, breath-gasping stance and stuck out my hand. I wanted to ask what AJ was short for but didn't want to come off as intrusive.

"Caleb," I said between breaths.

"Yeah. Didn't we have that one class together last semester?

"Nah, man. I'm just literally getting off the train. Just moved here."

"New kid! Nice," he said, taking one

30

of the duffels off my back and walking me
outside

"Hey man, do you know Brooklyn?" I
asked, nodding in her direction.

"Who, the new girl? Nah man, she moved
here last semester, I think. I heard she's
a bitch, though."

"Really?"

"Yeah, my friend Joelle tried talking
to her. I'll ask him again to see if I'm
remembering correctly."

When we walked out of the building, my
taxi driver from earlier was still out
front, waiting. He sat on the hood of his
car with a cocky grin on his face and my
laptop bag in hand.

"Friend of yours?" AJ asked.

"Yeah, something like that." I reached
in my pocket and grabbed my wallet in
defeat. I talked the taxi driver into
driving me to my grandma's by giving him
the money I owed him plus the new fare
upfront. AJ helped me get my bags into the
'taxi' and told me to meet him in the gym
in the morning before classes so he could
introduce me to some people.

For some reason, I couldn't shake the
thought of you-know-who. It got to be a
game where I tried not to say her name, but
sometimes I just couldn't help it.

Brooklyn.

We were both new in town, both in
Literary Arts 102. But she was, according

31

to AJ, a bitch. Because I couldn't shake her from my brain, that made the proverbial light bulb go off as if someone had pulled the beaded string attached to it in my head. The only explanation was I must be stuck in the matrix.

When I got to my grandma's, I saw that she was safely sleeping in her chair. This all came from looking in from the porch, through the screen door that was also unlatched. I was definitely not in Jersey anymore.

Letting myself in, I was able to set up my belongings in my Dad's old bedroom in peace without being micromanaged. Walking through the doorway to that room was like stepping out of a time machine into the 80s. Besides Father Time's fingerprint, everything was virtually untouched. When you walk in the room, the first thing you notice is the faded David Bowie poster. It sat between the two windows that looked out the front of the house. The walls had a stale tint to them and the paint had begun to crack. Under the poster was a tarnished metal desk that looked like it housed a neighborhood of spiders. The floors were coated in a dust that left prints when you walked across it.

Last but not least was where all the magic happened, or hopefully will happen: a twin-sized bed.

After I was finally finished putting

my stuff away, I went downstairs to see if my grandma had woken up.

"Who's there?" she cried out.

"It's me, grandma," I replied as I creaked down the old wood steps. I turned the corner to her holding a cast iron pan in a home run ready stance.

"Jesus, Grandma, it's Caleb!"

"Claaarrk! Hi, sweetheart. You can't answer 'it's me' when somebody asks who's there," she lectured while kissing me on my cheek as I leaned down to hug her. I forgot that she called me Clark from time to time. Her obsession with Seinfeld and pointing out every Superman placement was her thing. Maybe that's where I get my 90s obsession. In any case, her calling me Clark was really confusing for me as a kid. The older I got, the more the name annoyed me, which she found adorable, and so called me by it even more than before. I loved our bond.

"Note taken. How are you feeling?"

"How'd you get in the house?" she asked, dismissing my question as she walked past me into the living room. She dragged a small oxygen tank behind her that had a long tube looped under her nose. I felt a ball of guilt drop into my gut. I didn't know she needed an oxygen tank. The grandma I remember—

That thought alone, *the grandma I remember*, made me nauseous. How could I have such a large gap of memory for my own

33

grandmother? I tried to shake the self-condemnation, as if her being on oxygen was my fault for not preventing it in some way.

She removed the little tubes from her nose, turned the tank off, and left it beside the door. Then she walked across the room and sat by the window in a red leather chair. Finally, nostalgia! I remembered one Christmas when I was about four going with my parents into the city to pick out a present to send to Grandma.

During this trip, I got separated from my parents on the street. I had this white polar bear with a heart for a nose and a heart on all four paws. My Dad got it for me while he was away on business to Washington D.C., thus me naming him D.C. The streets were crowded, and someone's knee knocked the bear out of my hands. I turned behind me and watched another little girl pick him up and walk into a thrift store with her parents. Conveniently enough for me at that moment, my mother let my hand go to dig in her purse, so I walked back and followed the girl into the thrift store.

Following her around the store was a fun new game until I asked her to be my mommy and I the daddy, and she exploded in tears. Her parents whisked her away, kidnapping my new spouse and our adopted child. MY child. All I could do was cry. I was heartbroken.

34

The shop owner didn't know what else to do besides sit me in this big red leather chair and give me hot chocolate. My parents passed by the window, frantically searching for me, and doubled back when they saw me through the glass. The owner got off the phone to greet the hysterical couple, but seeing my mom and dad made me remember the thieving girl's rejection. Overcome with grief again, I spilled the cup of hot chocolate on the arm of the chair as I began to wail. The owner wasn't happy about that, and $200 later, grandma had her gift.

I could still vaguely see the brown stain on the arm of the chair. A stain of my first encounter of love at too early of an age. *Pfff* love.

Annoyed I didn't answer as fast as she liked, Grams cleared her throat to remind me of her question.

"Apparently people around here don't lock their doors, grandma," I said to her.

She ignored me now as she lit what seemed to be a joint, though she insisted it was only tobacco that she grew herself. It smelled an awful lot like weed, too. I really wanted to rant and rave about how bad smoking was for someone in her mysterious condition, let alone someone completely healthy and 100 years younger than her, but she stuck to her story, reminding me that she used to take care of

35

a community garden back in her prime. Despite me not seeing any gardens around, or her ability to maintain one, I just let it be.

Grams and I people-watched from the porch and talked until time got away from us. We talked about what new stuff was happening in the old neighborhoods she'd lived in back home, what stores were there and which weren't. We talked about how she goes to the doctor frequently and on which days. She let me know a bus comes by and picks up the elderly who can't drive, since the nearest hospital is forty minutes away.

Then we got into dissecting my life. Why I had no girlfriend and how I was going to find work, because the only person living under her roof unemployed was her. And then we spoke about the details of my parents' split.

I told her me not having a girlfriend stemmed from my parents' divorce (at least, that's what I told myself). I brokered a deal about not having a job because I wanted to focus on my career as a writer. Lastly, I told Grams about the girl I was seeing/dating getting engaged to her actual boyfriend. When I was telling the story, Grams couldn't hold back the tears—from laughing, of course. I'm not sure if it was the 'cigarettes' she was smoking, but she found everything I said to be hilarious. Then she did something I haven't experienced in such a long time. She did her Oracle thing.

"Sometimes the universe makes a mistake," she said. "The perfect stranger is out there that you share everything in common with, except for a time and place. Caleb, life is a string of chance encounters. Even with a billion-to-one odds, some encounters happen, and others don't. You never know how many things had to happen just to meet the one you love. Could have ended up on some other road in life because you missed your cue, or they missed theirs. Sure, you could still be telling yourself it was meant to be, and harp on it as if you knew all along. Or you will look back and say it was nothing personal, just a glitch in the…"

Grams paused while she had me on the edge of my seat. "What's that Sean Wick movie called?" she asked.

"*John Wick*," I laughed, "and it's *The Matrix*."

"Yeah, a glitch in the matrix," she said, satisfied with herself. Grams made it a point to try and know little things I am interested in so she 'didn't come off as an old woman.' I never really got a chance to talk about these things with my parents, so having someone actually willing to listen was nice for a change, even if they were laughing. I offered to help her to her room for the night and get her in bed, but she wanted to watch TV. She asked me to make myself useful and grab the remote off the coffee table. I turned on the TV and she instructed me to go into Hulu and put on *Seinfeld*.

"Forgive me and my old eyes, but I think it says last episode watched was three of season two, and you clicked episode six."

"Sorry. I wasn't paying attention."

"Imagine how lost I would have been, Caleb. Missing important lessons of their lives because of somebody else's mistake."

"Jesus, Grandma, it's a show. Sorry."

"Missing is worse than watching again. Even if I was to repeat something I already saw, it's okay. I may have a completely different take-away than before," she added.

The quirky theme music filled the room as I realized what Grams was saying wasn't filled with hostility over the show. It was her form of wisdom, wisdom that had nothing to do with Jerry, Elaine, or Kramer but everything to do with my parents and me. I sat the remote on the coffee table and began to retreat upstairs.

"Don't live your life avoiding mistakes your parents made. Sometimes you have to make them yourself before you can fully understand the lesson," she added, just in case I was too dense to get it.

"Love you too, Grandma."

CHAPTER FOUR

I sat in the gym the next morning,
exhausted. I had been up all night
listening to the muffled studio audience
laughter from the TV. Mainly what was on my
mind was the advice from my grandma. I'd
tossed and turned with her logic most of
the night.

*Make the mistakes other people made
because blah blah blah.* When I left this
morning, grandma was knocked out asleep in
the same chair I had left her in. I walked
her to her bed before I left and headed
over to the campus. This town was about ten
Manhattan city blocks, so walking around
was easy. Instead of buildings, it's a ton
of trees. Instead of concrete, it's grassy
and muddy paths.

It was nice having a change of scenery
for once. Taking it all in on my walk made
me forget about Jersey, which was also
nice. Even being here on campus has a
better feel than the colleges in the city.

I watched each person enter the gym,
hoping they were AJ—or at least that's who

I told myself I wanted it to be. Anyone who would rescue me from the judging eyes of the women setting up for their morning Zumba class would be appreciated. Just when I had decided to make an awkward escape, AJ appeared in the doorway.

"Yo, Caleb, come down here!" he yelled from the other side of the gym. I walked over to him, and he gave me an awkward, overly exaggerated handshake. We went across the hall to the lounge for breakfast, where I made my second friend, Joelle, or Jojo, as he preferred to be called. He had on a cartoon Albert Einstein graphic t-shirt, khaki cargo pants, and a pair of clean, black and white Vans. He tied the whole black hipster nerd look together with a pair of thick, forest green-framed glasses. In the midst of introductions, though, my attention was waltzed away when *she* passed by.

Brooklyn.

I waved at her, but she never quite looked in my direction so I tried to play it off as brushing away a gnat or something.

"See man, I told you she's a bitch," AJ said.

"Huh?"

"Dude, I saw you trying to get Brooklyn's attention."

"Ha! You're into her too?" Joelle laughed.

"Besides letting me share her book with her in class yesterday, it's all I know of her. I'm not *into her*," I said, ending my statement in air quotes.

"Maybe she's just one of those black chicks that isn't into white guys," Joelle shrugged.

"Dude, just because you are black doesn't mean you can rattle off statements like that," AJ fired back.

"Ninja, please," Joelle said in a roar of laughter.

"I'm not a white guy," I interjected.

"Soon as one of us gets a little tan, am I right?" AJ said. I left his hand hanging in the air from validation of his joke.

"Ethnically ambiguous, nice," Joelle added in between bites of his last tater tots.

"I don't think you used the word ambitious right, Jojo."

"Ambiguous, not ambitious. Anyway, didn't you try to date her, Jojo?" I asked him.

"NO!" he replied. "That was AJ. He probably just said that to seem like less of a loser because HE got rejected."

"Yeah, well, for starters I like older women and she's probably a lesbian," AJ defended himself while eating the last piece of food on Joelle's plate.

"Maybe she thinks she's better than

41

you both and has higher standards than either of you ball bags could meet," Joelle said, getting up to get more food. "All offense bro."

AJ replied with a middle finger.

"This is why relationships are more trouble than anything. What reasons do women have to be like that?" I mused, as a girl sat down in Joelle's spot and interjected into the conversation.

"Because we rule the world," she said.

"Caleb, this is JoJo's feminist girlfriend, Hillary Clinton."

She punched AJ in the arm and extended her hand to me. "Just Hillary is fine, or Hill." Funny thing about Hillary, she sort of looked like the former first lady when she was younger, just with better hair, minus the pants suits and cuter.

"Caleb," I replied, shaking her hand. I was still blanking on a cool alias or new name. Nine o'clock was approaching and the lounge started to slowly clear out. I had gotten to the school a bit earlier than I needed to so I could meet AJ and Joelle, so I had time to kill before my 10:30 am. Most of my classes this semester were for fun, more or less. I had taken additional classes my first year of college, and now I only needed the English credit to actually graduate.

My goal is to one day be a screenwriter/ director. Not in Hollywood, but in more of a Cannes-of-France-Film-Festival sense of the word. It's impossible for me to watch a movie or show and not want to critique it to what I deem is perfection. Because of my YouTube page, where I've uploaded a few film theories, I've even been able to land a job. It's a commissioned-based job where I critique films for a blog nobody has heard of, but it pays decently.

I walked into Dr. Valspar's class dreading whatever I felt coming towards me in the ethos. To my surprise, beside her desk was evidence she actually did have a human heart: a little dog.

Mut.

I assumed from the letters M-U-T engraved into a gold coin swinging from his collar it was probably both his name and his breed. The dog's coat was a mesh of patches with browns, grays and blacks. Three of his paws were solid white up to his knees while the fourth was solid black.

I thought the name was brilliant, in a "reclaiming it for my people" kind of way. Mut. Unlike other dogs that would normally jump up on you and force you to give them all of your attention, Mut seemed to not be interested in people. He was my spirit animal, or maybe from his point of view, I was his.

I wanted to pet him, but he looked at me with a look of exhaustion that I understood all too well, like seeing my own reflection. We were kindred spirits. Instead of invading his personal space, I sat across from him and nodded. He wagged his tail back at my nod, which I interpreted as a thanks for understanding.

I'm allergic anyway.

"Look at my good little boy, who's a good boy? Whosagooboy!" Valspar said, assaulting the puppy with baby talk. She bent down to pet him, ignoring my presence in the room. I could sense the annoyance she still had for me after waking up AJ yesterday evening.

Unintentionally, I cleared my throat.

"Is there something you need, Mr. Stevens?" she asked softly, but with poison in her tone.

"Just here for class," I answered cautiously.

"What is your major, Mr. Stevens?"

"General studies."

"Still figuring out life, then?" she asked. I wasn't sure if she was totally unmasking her displeasure with me, or simply amused by me.

"As much as a professor drinking wine at ten-thirty in the morning," I replied.

She stopped petting her dog and looked at me. She bit the bottom of her plum-stained lips for a moment, and then shot up and walked past me towards the back of the room. After rummaging through some papers, she walked back over to me and dropped a folder on my desk. She stood over me like a villain waiting on their moment to monologue as I shuffled through the papers.

"I assume since you are doing General Studies now you plan on transferring to a university later. My question was not only a personal attack on you but an actual inquiry for information," she said calmly.

"This is my work," she continued, handing me a large portfolio. "Since I Google every student I see on my roster for the semester, I know your potential. I want you to take my personal portfolio and choose five assignments from it. Execute them better than I did at your age, or you fail."

I had an urge to correct her regarding my degree, but I stopped flipping through the pages of the book as I noticed Mut rubbing against my leg. I dared not touch him and send his owner into a rage. Maybe he sensed how uncomfortable I was in this moment—or how turned on I was. I ignored it all.

"How come nobody else is here in class?" I asked, not acknowledging the workload she had almost literally dropped in my lap.

"Oh, Caleb," she said while twisting a nozzle on a box of wine hidden away in a closet. She poured some into her coffee cup and looked up with a smile. "Class starts at ten a.m. Normally at this campus, if a professor isn't in class within the first fifteen minutes, class is canceled. You are late for class, and your classmates have already left like I was hoping they would."

I looked back at my schedule and saw that a smudge had covered the zero, making me think it was a three. I stuffed her book under my arm and stood up to leave.

"And where do you think you are going, young man?" But her tone said she didn't really care.

"To have lunch with my grandmother. I have time to kill until my next class and I wanted to surprise her with some food."

"You have a lot to learn about women, Mr. Stevens," she laughed while kicking her feet up onto her desk. "Always late, responding to the tension in a woman's voice, and getting her food without asking what she is in the mood for first? Good luck."

This was a test. One I was willing to fail, but I swallowed my pride.

"Door open or closed, Professor Valspar?"

"Closed," she said, placing a magazine over her face to rest. I didn't close the door. Even though I felt a small victory in that moment, I also felt I was somehow proving her point.

I stopped at a grocery store that was near the school to grab some food. I walked through the doors and strolled the aisles thinking if I should cook or not. The aroma from the deli drew me in, pulling me to the case of hot wings. I got three different flavors with four different sauces to dip them in, taking Valspar's advice into consideration. Even if Grandma weren't in the mood for chicken, she would still have options to choose from.

I had wasted too much time at the grocery store, so I jogged back to Gram's. When I got there, I must have just missed her weed man, because there were a few pill bottles with already rolled joints in them. At least she doesn't know how to break down the weed and roll them herself, I thought, looking for a silver lining. We ate chicken from the grocery store deli and watched *Maury*. In the midst of 'you are not the fathers' and infomercials I had to talk my grandma into not ordering from, she asked me the inevitable.

"When are you having a kid?"

"When I can afford to buy one off the black market."

"You mean adopt? That's very un-American."

"I feel like that's a really American thing, actually, and no, I didn't mean adopt. I was making a joke."

"Well, I want grandkids, Caleb." I

could tell she was being serious because she used my actual name.

"I am your grandkid, grandma," I laughed. "You have to lay off the ciga-weed."

"Don't make fun of old people for being senile. You are gonna get old one day too, you know."

I checked my watch, stood up and popped the last piece of chicken in my mouth.

"Nah, grandma, I'm not getting old. I'm gonna die before that happens."

She laughed and jabbed me in my ribs while I bent down to kiss her. As I walked back to school, I caught myself smiling for no reason. But the more I thought about it, the reason was clear.

My grandma.

She was like a stranger that I knew and trusted and could let my guard down around. It sucks it took her getting sick for me to reconnect with her, but better late than never. A nasty taste formed in my mouth for even considering calling Grams a stranger. Sometimes it annoyed me how much my brain thought in 'moral of the story' form. People say things happen for a reason. I think it's more true that things happen and people assign reasons to them.

I just do it consciously.

I walked through the doors of campus and checked my watch to make sure that my timing wasn't off.

"Hey, new kid!" a voice said from behind me. I turned to see her standing there.

Brooklyn.

"New kid, aye? Aren't you technically new, too?" I replied with a smile. The smile was for being impressed with myself for how quick I thought on my feet.

"Oh, has somebody been doing their research on little ole me?"

I laughed to mask my embarrassment and frustration.

"The streets talk," I said, with another awkward laugh after hearing how dumb 'streets talk' sounded out loud.

"Oouu, big bad Jersey boy," she mocked. She smiled and snapped both of her fingers up and down while methodically walking backwards into her classroom. Even though she just shamelessly did a mini *Grease* number into class, I couldn't help feeling like the bigger goof.

"Streets talk," I repeated to myself. It didn't dawn on me until she left that she must have done some research too, because I didn't tell her I was from Jersey.

CHAPTER FIVE
(**155mi**)

I've been awake for a while now. The branches from the tree beside my house tapped on the window, as if they were trying to get my attention. I was dreaming. I don't really remember much about the dream now, but I know it was good because I was smiling when I opened my eyes. I tried to fall back asleep, but soon after a symphony of lawnmowers started up and well, I've just been laying here.

After a while, I figured out why I was woken up. I'm being haunted. Haunted by nostalgia. Funny enough, I'm even suffering from a sort of sleep paralysis too. I'm not even sure what time it is.

I watched the shadows of the bare trees dance over my shoulder and across my comforter, glide over my slippers lying on the floor, and shimmy up the wall. I used that time lapse like some sort of abstract sundial, and figured it was almost noon now.

Usually I love sleeping in, but today my brain went back to the last time I had

50

this luxury, and well, the feeling wasn't as sweet as it used to be.

Funny, you take something you've always loved doing and share it with a person. Now that 'something' feels ten times better than it ever was before. But as soon as that person isn't there anymore, that same something you always loved is sort of soured. Everything can be back to the way it was before them, but it will never be the same—

The branches tapping on the window again made me lose my train of thought. The shadows swayed back and forth on my wall like brittle fingers, pointing to the top of my dresser. What was ominously waiting at the end where I was being directed? Two movie tickets for a film I've been obsessing over for a few weeks.

I had planned to go with a certain someone to see this movie, and now the universe was—more mocking than haunting me, I guess. Another something good, soured. That's why I've been laying here, unable to move. I feel like I've been using all my strength and energy brainstorming my conundrum. Should I wait for the movie to come out on Netflix to watch it, or should I go and see it, and spend some time with myself instead of just inside my own head.

I kicked the sheets off of me and got ready. I would take myself on this date just like old times when I lived back home.

Vagiant 2: Half vampire, Half giant, whole human heart.

The title had me sold on the movie as soon as I saw the poster for it in the subway back home, and I bought two tickets after I saw the trailer. I think I was at the movies alone when I saw that trailer, too. Of course I had made plans, but I knew my friends wouldn't show up. That's just how they were. With them often flaking on me, leaving me to do things alone, I'd learned I do enjoy my own company.

And just like that, I could breathe again. If I had to describe it, it's like a smoker's first cigarette after good sex. That exhale of, 'Yeah, I just did that.'

Or something really close to that, anyway. Leaving the movie theater was like taking a first breath, not realizing I had been drowning before. How tight my chest was, how deafening everything could be around me, arms tired of flailing trying desperately to reach the surface.

I'm fine now. I mean, sure I thought I was fine before, but this remedy always did the trick. I just needed to spend some time with myself, instead of inside my own head. What better way to do that than to take yourself on a date?

I even surprised myself with food from a day before that I had forgotten I had saved in my jacket pocket. Chicken nuggets. And I have so many theories about this movie I can throw on my YouTube channel! I feel inspired to upload again since my *Blair Witch* video. That's why I can't wait to get home after that movie.

"Sounds like you have pretty shitty friends," the woman said to me. I forgot where I was for a second. I looked up from my chocolate milk on the table over to the woman beside me. Her facial expression read, "Kill Me." As if I was boring her to death with my story.

"Sorry. Forgot where I was. I didn't even realize I was talking out loud. Distracted I guess. How much did you hear?"

"Something about chicken nuggets. I don't know, look." She moved the plate of cake out of my lap, pushing over my glass of milk, and straddled me. "I'll be your distraction," she continued. "I'll help you forget about being friendless or whatever."

"I have friends, ma'am. The ones in Jersey were maybe more casual than I realized, but my friends now though are pretty great. They're the reason I'm here instead of going home."

"Well, are they gonna bring you over some money so I can dance and get the hell out of here?"

"Actually…" I trailed off, pulling out my phone. I swiped around and showed her my screen. Somehow AJ had got a coupon called 'Heaven: Buy one slice of cake and get 7 minutes FREE with an Angel!'

He said he would kill me if I didn't go, and that their chocolate cake was to die for, so here I am. She slowly climbed off my lap while zooming in to read the fine print. She jiggled the door handle, and sighed when she saw it was locked. Then the woman magically pulled a cell phone out of thin air after reaching into the crotch of her white lace leotard and showed me a timer counting down from four minutes. Looking around the five-by-five room, I noticed that it was glass from the ceiling down until it switched to sheetrock about where your shoulders would be if you were sitting on the couch. That's when I realized this was a sexy closet, and got the clever title of the coupon. The bass from whatever song was bleeding through the frosted glass and awkward silence filled the room.

"So, what's distracting you? Your wife?" she said, grasping for straws.

"Pff, wife. No."

"Well, it has to be a girl, that's the only reason people come in here."

"Clearly it's not," I said, pointing at the cake again. The woman then stuck her finger in the middle of it while calling me an asshole under her breath. She sat back again and crossed her arms.

Suddenly there was a knock on the glass. Another stripper was pointing at her head, which made the girl reach in the

54

cushion of the couch and put on a halo. I began to laugh, until I felt the look of death on me. She did a deep exhale and started to unbuckle the strap on her white high heels.

"I guess I am in here because of a girl," I admitted. "To forget one, rather."

"Which is why you went to the movies alone."

"Bingo," I said, taking a lonely sip of the last of my chocolate milk. The girl did another exhale and stood up. She then leaned over me, placed the halo on my head and started dancing slowly.

"Oh you don't hav—"

She placed her finger over my mouth and straddled me again. I didn't notice before how much she smelled like vanilla and honey. I kept my hands to my side as her hips rocked back and forth, making the front of my jeans tighter and tighter. I tried to look at the timer on the table to see how long before I could get out of here, but she was blocking it.

"So," she said, with a whole new tone of lust in her voice. "Was that movie you went to see a porn?"

"*Vagiant*?" I paused for a moment until I realized how the title could give her that idea. "Oh no. It's a movie about a vampire who's a giant, but he's not really a giant. It's just everybody around him is like five-six and he's six-eleven, so the

55

other Vampires treat HIM like he's better than everyone but he doesn't treat THEM like he feels that way. And I have a film theory that—"

She covered my lips with her finger again, stopping my nervous ramblings.

"Is that your wallet, or are you happy to see me finally."

"It's my wallet," I lied, embarrassed.

"Good. Take out your… wallet," she commanded with a whisper to my ear.

"I have to go." I laughed nervously.

"Why?" she exhaled.

"My film theory." I was totally in the moment now. I slid my hands down the back of her silky skin.

"What's your name?"

"Caleb."

"Hi, Caleb, I'm London."

I stopped immediately. The timer went off and somehow my wallet was in her hand.

"Okay, time to go," I told her.

"Don't worry about the timer. I just have to swipe—"

"Nope. Not swiping anything. I gotta go." I pushed her off me on to the couch, then stood up and knocked on the glass for the door to be unlocked.

"What the hell, man. I thought we were having fun."

I ignored her as another girl with angel wings in her hand came over to the door. "Hand me your card for the upgrade and I will give you the wings," she said.

"No, thank you. I'm going home. Unlock the door please."

The woman looked at the girl on the couch, confused. She finally opened the door and I pushed past her. I walked a few steps before something inside me made me turn back to ask, "Is that really your name?"

"London? Yeah, so?"

"And have you ever bee-"

"No, I've never been, never even been to Europe."

With the overwhelming taste of nostalgia in my mouth I didn't even bother responding. I walked over to the counter and waited for them to ring my card for the cake.

"So," the bartender said too enthusiastically for my blood. "Did you enjoy your night in London?"

I snatched my card, ignoring how clever the pun was.

"No, I'm afraid of heights?" I said, wishing I could have come back with something equally as witty. I grabbed another slice of cake off the counter and left feeling good about my late game victory. I walked down a few blocks and ordered an Uber and took a bite of the cake, only to spit it out realizing it was carrot cake. I canceled the car and decided to walk home while laughing at the earworm in my head.

"A night in London."

CHAPTER SIX

My eyes were heavy. They had started
to sting from me resisting defeat. I was
determined to not let this thing beat me. I
stared stubbornly, trying to keep my eyes
open until my reflection was blurred from
tears I couldn't hold back any longer. All
that was there was nothing.

I let the void engulf me until I could
imagine myself walking around the emptiness
that plagued me. The nothingness was
blinding and somehow also deafening. Only
the sound of the occasional car passing by
outside my window reminded me that I was
still connected to something. Reminding me
I was still present in some sort of
reality. A reality with so much to give,
and so much to say. Instead, this reality
rejected me. Offering me nothing, reminding
me that I was nothing.

A backfire from one of those passing
cars forced me out of the moment. I
blinked. Somehow, me deciding to force
myself to sit down and write had turned
into a staring contest. Yes, a staring

contest with this stupid blank screen.

What did I think? Maybe if I win, the words will just write themselves? First it had to blink, and I was fighting a battle against writer's block I've lost all too often before. I wiped the tears from my face, regretting the grasp at straws. I was desperate to try and get a win, regardless of how little or insignificant. I needed that.

That's when a light bulb went off above my head. I decided to use these thoughts during my "battle" and actually write them down.

"Caleb: One, Writers Block:…"

I decided maybe I wouldn't admit that actual score, since the history of me on the losing end was lengthy. I decided to just take my small victory for what it was, at least that's what Grams would say.

"Someone's finally alive!" Grandma shouted, tone deaf to the fact that she didn't actually have to yell over the music in her headphones.

"Speak of the Devil."

"What?" she continued.

"I said speak of the—" I cut myself off and just motioned for her to remove her headphones.

She finally shuffled passed me and made her way to her red leather chair. "You are writing again, Clark! Oh, that's good to see, good to see!" she continued.

I smiled with a yawn. My body must be still trying to adjust from the movies the other night after weeks of being glued to my bed.

"Oh, wait until I have my headphones out, Clark, before you start talking."

"Grams, I didn't say anything."

"Yeah, I didn't hear you say anything."

"No," I laughed, "I wasn't saying anything. I just yawned Grams, that's it."

"Wearing all that black still," she said immediately with disapproval, moving on to her next thought. I loved how her brain worked. If she got bored or didn't care what you were saying, then she'd be on to the next. If she was to ask how you were doing and you took it for anything other than being polite, and actually started to tell her, she would rush right in to get straight to the point of it all. "I thought maybe you were finally over yourself," she continued.

"Well, I'm in mourning," I replied.

"You aren't mourning any damn thing."

"I'm not?" I asked stoping my typing to defend myself. She shook her head while she watched a honeybee out the window. "It's noon and I just got out of bed, I've been moping around, the all black-"

"Laziness," She said simply.

"Lazy?" I laughed.

"When you were a kid all you did was

60

sit around. I told your folks it was
probably polio but they just called me
crazy and you la-"

"Polio!?" I yelled as I waited for her
to laugh, but she was serious. I continued
to make my case, "I stopped writing for a
while, I've been drinking a bunch, and-"

"I heard about your little AA meeting
situation a few weeks ago." She
interrupted. I pretended to go back to
typing as if I didn't hear her. She cleared
her throat and I could feel her flash me a
stern look.

"From who, JoJo?"

"No, AJ came over to check on me the
other night because he said you would be
out late after he gave you a coupon."

"AJ? For real?" I puzzled.

"No, for pretend, Mr. Director," She
poked fun, "What was it he said you were
trying to do again?" she thought out loud.
Grams love to repeat jokes or anything she
thought was slightly amusing from younger
people.

"Getting old," I mumbled.

"Older the berry the sweeter the
juice," she laughed. I couldn't help but
laugh with her and how much this woman and
I amused each other. I've felt like I
wanted to ask where she's been all my life,
but I know the answer. She's been here, a
train ride away, a phone call away even.
But there's always been a way.

"If you say so Grams."

"Exactly, and I say you aren't mourning any damn thing. You are just acting out and showing your tail, drinking and sleeping all day because you feel it's how you are supposed to act."

"I feel that's how I'm supposed to act?"

"Yeah. Instead of just feeling it. You listed everything as if you are purposely doing it."

"Purposely?" My only reactions to what Grams was saying was to repeat what things she said. If wasn't intentional, more like my brain was stalling for the proper defense. The bee finally floated away and she turned her attention to me again.

"At least you are writing again. Eyes all red tough, must be crying a letter to that girl." she baited.

'*Crying a letter?*' I repeated to myself, but out loud I didn't bite. She reached for one of the pill bottles on her table I was borrowing. I was shocked she wasn't fussing at me for using it as my desk, but I guess she chose to spare me after already leaning into me. She unscrewed the top of the bottles one after the other—they were all empty. She reached for another on the windowsill by her chair, and that was empty too.

"Out of your meds?" I laughed, steadily typing away, trying to not let my previous thoughts escape me. Without missing a beat, she reached behind the chair to grab the cane she never used for walking. I was convinced it was strategically placed there for one reason only, to hit me when I was bothering her.

"Okay," I surrendered to her with a laugh.

Grams placed the back of her hand over her brow in a dramatic damsel fashion. She cleared her throat and started fanning herself with the other hand. "Oh, Clarky," she said in a distressed, 1960s falsetto voice. "I need my meds. Why, what ever shall I do without them?"

"Look here, toots," I joined in the charade, "I'll call the pharmacy for you, but that's where I draw the line, see. I'm not calling that two-bit son of a gun over here for no more home deliveries, see. He's no good for yous."

"Oh, that old boy? I haven't seen him in a dog year. I'm sure he's changed. I need the good stuff, Clarky, the good stuff."

"A dog year? I win," I said, breaking character.

"It's a thing, I think. Besides, you sound like the sandwich guy from over on Main Street. I win."

"Who, Tony?"

"Yup, and I heard he's been mixed up in some trouble. I don't want you going over there."

"You have nothing to worry about on that," I said, unintentionally somber. My tone caused Grams to whip her head around and look at me squinty-eyed.

"Good," she said, gripping her cane again. "Now, answer my question about these tears."

"I haven't been crying," *Not today at least,* I thought. "I was staring at the screen until I got some sort of inspiration to write and the white light was burning my eyes. And it's not a love letter."

"Okay, so read it to me."

"No. It's really nothing," I protested. It didn't matter to her. She pulled the table I was typing on away from me towards her. She flipped my laptop around, took off the glasses from the top of her head and placed them in the neck of her shirt.

"Grams." I laughed at her choosing to grab her glasses but not put them on. She shushed me as if my talking was impacting her sight. Her eyes squinted and scanned over my random thoughts, and she shook her head as she read.

"Reminding me that I was nothing," she said, reading the last sentence out loud. "Do not send that to Brooke."

"I'm not. I was brainstorming and then a staring contest, and I don't know…"

"Staring contest with yourself." She

64

was famous for stating questions but not really looking for answers. Of course, I always answered anyway.

"Yes."

"I mean, it's good baby. Dramatic, but good. You have to really take your victories for what they are, no matter how big or small," she said, sending a grin over my face. "Well, I want to laugh, too," she added.

"It's nothing," I said, closing the laptop.

I watched her as she looked out the window. Grandma always looked like she had something on her mind. That thought had always been funny to me, because she's never been one to hold her tongue and the first to speak her mind. She says it's because she's an Aries, whatever that means. As long as I've known Grams, she never was a religious person. Mainly stars, the moon, energy and the universe-type person, but not religious per se. Sure, she'd always watch the programs and listen to the music. But I find, more recently, that she's looked up at the sky a lot.

"What's on your mind?" I asked her. She didn't answer immediately, which made me think she was contemplating telling me something or not. Not my Grams, I assured myself, she wouldn't keep a secret from me. She was so good at reading my mind, but I could never read hers.

"I'm trying to remember something I heard on one of those talk radio episode things," she answered after a while.

"A podcast?"

"Yeah, I think so. I was listening to something about the CD Universe and Superman and woke up to them talking about women and refrigerators and I think I want to do that for your story."

I sat looking at her confused, trying to decipher what the hell she was talking about. I figured she meant DC Universe when she mentioned Superman, but the rest was pure nonsense.

"Either you don't need any more of that medicine or you need therapy, Grams."

"You know, I used to be a therapist, Caleb," she said.

"A therapist, grandma? Really?"

"Yes. They didn't really want black women to be in that field, or women in general, but I was making a name for myself. It's not always what you know; it's also who you know."

"You saying I need therapy, grams?" She didn't answer. She looked me up and down, from my black Nike slides and black socks to my black sweats and black t-shirt. She smiled and went to looking back out the window at her honey bee friend.

"Did you turn your shirt inside ou—"

"Yeah yeah," I interrupted. "I don't own an all-black shirt so I turned my

Smiths tour shirt inside out."

"You kids know nothing about being emo, or the Smiths for that matter." Grams stood up and made her way over to the sofa. She plopped down and slowly lifted her legs onto the cushions. She folded her hands and motioned to me.

I walked over and sat in the recliner facing her.

"Aren't I supposed to be the one laying down?"

"Wish they would have let me take you to get looked at." She mumbled as she tossed a blanket over my lap. I laughed embracing the look.

"Now, what are you mourning?"

"I mean…" My mind went blank after those two words and I clammed up. I'm sure she knew the answer, but I felt like she was asking something else, something deeper. I went to fix my mouth to say her name, but Grams shot me a look of 'don't you dare,' confirming my suspicions. I thought longer on the question. If I wasn't mourning Brooklyn, what was I mourning?

What we had?

What we were?

Was it all of the above?

"I don't know," I answered finally.

"Exactly," she said, sitting up with a grin. She slipped on her slippers and tried to suppress a laugh.

"Real funny, Grams. No wonder your

career never took off."

"Believe it or not, I helped you just now, Caleb, and you will be better off thanking me now and not when I give you something to mourn about," she said, shaking her little fist at me. "I was helping people by making them tell me what they already knew. People are too fast to answer questions. Just listen, reflect and then answer. Coming up with the answer on your own makes people feel better. Makes them feel like they don't need me, but they do."

"How short were your sessions?"

"About as long as this one. Maybe longer since those people had real problems." She finished with chucking a pillow at me with a smile.

"Did these people ever come back?"

"Yes."

"So, what the hell happened?"

With that, I opened the floodgates. Grams was the best storyteller. I never knew what parts were facts or fiction, but I always got the sense the story was real. She told me how she was working as a secretary in a loft building in downtown Manhattan. The building was a grand, ten-story beauty down in Soho, where the entire floor was open to whatever squatters, asbestos, and—lucky for her—entrepreneur types wanted to use it. On Grams's floor there was an acupuncturist, a fortuneteller, a yoga class, community garden, seamstress, a therapist, and a Campbell's Soup painter. Grams hadn't gone to school because she thought it was a scam. She always knew she wanted to own her own business, so she volunteered her secretarial services, which turned into a paid gig after a few days and deciding to collect a small fee from each spot at the end of the week. This, of course, turned into a lecture of going after what you want and not letting anybody get in your way.

Advice I feel like she gave that got me in my heartbreak predicament.

After I got her back on track to the original story, she told me she noticed that the therapist started to show up less and less after his engagement was called off. If for any reason he did decide to show up, he would reek of Jameson and pass out in one of the massive window frames. Grams said she didn't like seeing people in need be turned away (and yes, that's the part of the story so far that I didn't believe), so that's when she started to step up and talk with people.

It was weird at first, she admitted. Seeing people pour out their hearts to a stranger for some sort of relief. In her house growing up, she told me, Great Grams and Gramps never talked about their emotions, which was reminiscent of my own parents.

Once these people started coming back to see her, she hired her own assistant to handle the other businesses. It became a needed therapy for herself too, even if a majority of it was just listening. Sometimes people just need someone to talk to.

After a while, customers started to pay her in cash upfront instead of dropping checks in the mailbox. Grams had gotten tired of helping people, then watching the drunk man come and collect checks off of her work. One day he showed up and the mailbox was empty. He accused Grams of stealing from him and tried to have her fired. He had forgotten that the entire floor was being run as smooth as it was because of Grams, and that she had turned her freelance secretary job into a makeshift management company.

Even so, because she was the only person of color in the building, she thought it would be safer if she left and never went back. She took that money and bought a townhouse in Jersey. Then my dad's sperm donor, as Grams puts it, came by not too long after and left even sooner than that.

"And you somehow still believe in love?" I asked her.

"Well, it was love that gave me the opportunity to discover my emotions when that smart woman left that drunk therapist.

It was love for your father that made me realize it was best your grandfather left and not come back, and it was love that brought your mom along to save your knucklehead father. And they gave me you, so yes, I believe in it. You know what I say about signs."

"Stop at them if they are red."

"Funny."

"I know, I know. You have to know when to read the signs. I'm just really bad at it."

"Exactly. Signs of what's good love and what's bad love, and when to let love go."

"And if it's real love, it will come back?"

"We are talking about love, Clark, not Frisbee. You need to get out more. Date again. There's a nurse at my—"

"Fine, fine," I said, trying to drown out her never-ending list of things I needed to be doing. I walked over and kissed her on the forehead.

"Love's complicated, Clark, and—"

"I know, Grams. But it's supposed to be. Right? At least, that's what I've been told."

She looked at me for a second. As if she was reading me to see if I believed my own words. I didn't.

"Lunchtime?" she asked, finally breaking the silence.

"Yes, ma'am." I walked over to the door and opened it.

"Clark, a jacket, please. It's windy out there," she protested.

"It's super warm out, Grandma. I'll be fine," I replied, opening the door.

"Caleb," she said softly. I closed the door and went to run upstairs and grab a hoody. "Behind the door in the closet right there, honey. I'm starving, now stop wasting time," she added.

I looked at the jacket and shook my head with a smile. I grabbed it off the hook and went outside.

"Love you," she said with a laugh lingering in her tone. I waved back, smiling in defeat as I put on the very colorful green and white windbreaker jacket that stopped mid forearm. It must have been there since my dad lived here. *I love you too Grams,* I said to myself.

CHAPTER SEVEN
(1,737mi)

On Fridays my grandma has doctors appointments all day, which she forbid me to attend, so I actually went to the computer lab to finish my sandwich for a while on campus.

While I was there, the intercom tone went off.

"Pardon the interruption," Betty White's voice came over the loudspeaker for an announcement. "Will all the students attending Dr. Valspar's class this semester please report to the annex building at this time."

I felt as if Betty and Valspar met to conspire against me. Before I could take a bite of my food, the tone went off again. I stood up before she could repeat herself. I walked into the hall and turned the corner to see Hillary and friends walking through the doors at the other end. I followed them to the annex. When we walked in, the dean was in the middle of a speech.

"—so from this day on, your two art classes will be combined. Dr. Valspar no

73

longer works here, and if you guys want a new vending machine and tires for the campus security cart, then we can't afford to hire anyone else without depleting the budget. That is all."

The announcement seemed oddly personal, as he could have posted this on the online portal for Blackboard, or even a sticky note on the door. Hillary mouthed and nodded to me from across the room. I had no idea what she was trying to tell me, so I gave her a thumbs up and left.

I was fortunate that AJ, Hillary and Brooklyn's classes ended around the same time as mine. Although I was usually done for the day, I hung around in the lounge and ate with them before they had their next classes.

"Are you lost, Jersey boy?" Brooklyn said.

"No, Brooklyn girl, I am not. This is my lunch. I just didn't skip it today."

"I'm not from Brooklyn."

"Really?"

"Nope. Never even been to New York before. My mom just loved the name."

"That's weird, why would your mom do that?" AJ asked.

"Because women can do whatever we want," Hillary answered.

"You sort of remind me of Brooklyn," I said. There was a pause and everyone looked at me. AJ mouthed to me that I was an idiot, but neither of the girls noticed. "You'd have to see it to know what I mean," I tried to explain myself. "A pretty cool place is what I mean." I finished stumbling over my word vomit.

"Well, I'm more than just cool. I'm a pretty dope girl," Brooklyn said, smiling at me as I tried not to make eye contact.

"Well, Stevens here is a recovering addict," AJ said while I kicked him in the shin. I regretted telling him about my twelve-step program days, now, because I didn't think he really understood what I was doing.

"Guys," Hillary said eagerly, "you know how Dr. Valspar is a lesbian?"

Everyone nodded but me.

"She was?"

"Not was, is," Hillary corrected me.

"Yeah, dude. Degeneresly gay," AJ joked. Hillary glared at him.

"I'll allow it," she said. "Only because rumor has it she was caught fooling around with a staff member in the bathroom one morning and only one of them got fired. Somebody complained she was never in class."

"That can't be real," Brooklyn said.

"No. I was in that class. She was never there," I replied, adding my two cents as if I had attended more than five classes.

"Dude. Do you know Frenchy is gay?" AJ

asked, hung up on the fact that I was clueless about Dr. Valspar.

"The foreign exchange student? No, he's just French, right?"

"Dude, really?" AJ said, pointing. I turned and saw Frenchy making faces into a pocket mirror.

"Oh, big deal. The guy can't make sure he doesn't have food in his teeth?"

"No," Hillary said, "look again."

I turned and noticed he wasn't just making faces, but was making faces in the mirror at the janitor polishing a pole behind him. And the janitor seemed to be enjoying it.

"Okay, yeah, well, I don't have gaydar. Besides, who cares if somebody is gay? You thought Brooklyn was a lesbian."

"What?" Brooklyn shouted at AJ.

"We still can't disprove those facts," he replied.

"I'm just really bad at reading signs. Trust me," I repeated.

"You should work on that," Brooklyn said with a smile, for now lets go over some stuff for class."

"You guys have fun." Hillary prompted as she pulled AJ up out of his seat leaving us alone.

"So…" I said awkwardly into the silence.

"So." Brooklyn smirked as she pulled out the textbook I have yet to go to the bookstore and get.

"They should do a course on Valspar next semester and her romance on Campus."

"Yeah. Poor Valspar. We could learn a lot." She said flipping through pages.

"Poor Valspar? That woman was all drama."

"She was afraid to love whenever where ever. It's admirable. Besides, there are such things as good drama and bad drama."

"Oh I gotta hear this." I said dragging the chair closer. I propped my elbows on the table and rested my chin on my fist, giving her my full attention.

"Okay," she smiled amused at my challenge, "lets take the story at hand here for example."

"Romeo and Juliet? Your argument is going to defend my point without me breaking a sweat."

"It's one of the most iconic love stories of all time! Even death can not defy love." She said satisfied.

"You're crazy."

"I'm crazy?" she laughed.

"You, Juliet, Romeo, all crazy. It's one of the most iconic stories of the most socially accepted form of crazy, which is the perfect way to define love."

I started to wonder if I maybe laid it on too thick until she challenged me again.

"Do you think it's possible to have a shitty step mother and step siblings?"

"Yeah?"

"Do you think that girl could go to a party, find a guy she's a perfect fit for, and then she move away with him from her abusive family?"

"Sure. Are you okay? Are you trying to tell me somethi-"

"No genius pay attention," she laughed, "So you think it's possible for them to run off and live happily ever after?"

"Oh okay," I laughed, "Yes if you phrase it like that with out the fairy god mother, yes Cinderella is possible."

"So you agree with me that fairytales are possible. That's all I wanted."

"Okay but-"

"No buts." She cut me off as Hillary came back and sat at the table.

"Why does Caleb look like he has egg on his face?" Hillary asked.

"Hillary how long did you wait on your prince charming before you got with Joelle?" I asked her, grasping for rope in my argument.

"Hell, I'm still waiting." She joked.

"Damn right girl. And Caleb I'm not waiting on one, I am Prince Charming." Brooklyn said as they dug deeper into a whole other conversation.

Since the mentioning of egg on my face, I didn't stay long after realizing I had forgotten my debit card at Gram's

house. I had wanted to be home when Grams
got there anyway, so the fact I had no
money to buy food kept me to my commitment.
I had planned to try and get some
information out of the nurses dropping her
off, but I couldn't remember the exact time
she got back. That's when I realized my
phone was dead. I went to the office to see
if I could use their phone to call the
hospital. I could have went back and asked
Hillary or Brooklyn to use their phones but
I wanted to avoid looking like I just
wanted an excuse to see Brooklyn again. I'm
sure I was just in my own head about it,
but I dismissed it.

I was taken aback by the brighter mood
in the office. Betty wasn't there, so
things were jollier. Even the people
leaving the financial-aid office were
smiling, as if the fossil behind the desk
was approving loans just because he was in
good spirits.

As I fumbled in my pockets for the
paper with the doctor's number on it, I
wondered if it had been Valspar and Betty
fooling around and shuddered at the
thought. The office was still empty, and I
listened as a phone rang and rang until a
fax machine screamed a binary laugh in my
ear.

I gave up using the phone and turned
to the window to see AJ performing some
sort of mime routine on the other side of

the glass, trying to get my attention. When I walked out into the hall, he swung his arm around my neck.

"Dude, she's into you," he said.

"Who?"

"Brooklyn!"

"She said those words, or are you assuming?"

"She basically said it, which counts all the same."

"Basically," I mocked him. "Dude, whatever. I'm here to take care of my grandma and-"

"And enjoy a new life away from the city," he said, cutting me off. "What better way to enjoy life than to fall in love?"

I started to think maybe I wasn't as in my head about Brooklyn as I thought when I saw the Dean storming down the hall. I wanted to ask him about one of my credits not carrying over—and get away from AJ's line of questioning—so I followed him. He burst through the doors angrily and I slowed, unsure if I should continue to chase him down. Then, I heard some arguing on the other side of the door, and the Jersey city boy in me couldn't help but try and listen.

Of course, as only I would, I leaned on the door a bit too hard, causing it to swing open. I caught the end of some quarrel, and it felt like I really was back in Jersey, with this scene hitting a little too close to home. I watched the Dean jump in his truck and speed off as the head librarian turned and saw me standing like a deer in headlights. She lit a cigarette and walked past me to stand by the door. I turned to her to try and fill the air with something other than despair, like I used to with my mom, but she cut me off as if she read what I was going to do next.

"What did you need with my husband?"

"Husband? I didn't know you and the dean were married?"

"I didn't take his last name," she said as I nodded my head, pretending I remembered any of their names. "And was married," she added.

"Excuse me?"

"Exactly how much of that did you hear, Mr.…?"

"Caleb. And nothing I haven't experienced with my own parents."

She smiled softly, almost as if she was relieved with my answer. "He's probably gonna divorce me after what happened today," she sighed.

That's when it all hit me like a ton of bricks, like somebody had changed the channel to a soap opera. Dr. Valspar got fired for fooling around with Mrs. Salloway, and Salloway kept her job because she's married to the dean.

"This is why I avoid relationships," I

81

said under my breath.

"No, you can't avoid love all your life. That's not living," she responded.

"Why not? Love is complicated," I said, turning around. I leaned against the door to look at her. She was staring off towards the right of the parking lot. I looked to see two birds chasing each other over the baseball field below. She lit another cigarette and blew the smoke into the sky.

"Good," she said. "Love is supposed to be complicated." She took another pull and blew more smoke. "Because if it's too simple, you have no reason to try and be happy. And if you don't have a reason to try, then you won't be happy." The birds flew around the corner of the school out of our view. I'm not sure if she had further proved my point about how pointless relationships were, or if she had made me feel pointless for always avoiding them.

"That was deep," I told her as she turned and opened the door to the school.

"I might have heard it falling asleep watching a movie or something."

"What movie?" I asked as we walked down the hall.

"Can't remember. Come, I'll walk you to your class so you're not tardy," she said, tossing an elbow into my side.

"Huh?"

"Sorry," she laughed nervously, "I was

getting after-school special vibes just now. I make poor jokes in awkward moments," she said with a smile.

I understood all too well. If I had been scripting this, it's where the message of this episode would have gone. She was distracted and trying to deflect, but I could tell she understood that I wasn't going to tell anyone about her and Valspar. Salloway was just too nice for any of that, a rare case of a genuinely nice person. She was actually the complete opposite of her counterpart—or parts for that matter.

It's funny, because even with everything she was going through, she was positive about it all. Funniest part about it all was I thought the Dean was still lucky to have her.

The irony.

CHAPTER EIGHT

It's been two weeks, and I have somehow exceeded my expectations. Survival was top priority, but I've managed to somehow feel like I belong. Everything felt familiar, even if it was all happening for the first time. It was great, but I needed more, something new, inspiration to write.

I walked in the gym to catcalls from Joelle and AJ playing a two-on-three men versus women game. I tried to pretend to not hear them while I stopped and asked to borrow a kid's homework for my abnormal psych class. I told myself leaving Jersey I would leave behind my bad habits also, but nobody's perfect.

I wasn't a bad student, a B- kind of guy, actually. I just always felt like I could be doing something more productive with my time. After graduating, I did semesters here and there at whatever school would take my financial aid. My transcript has been through so many different schools that I don't care to even walk the stage next year—just email me my degree. I'd always envied staying in a dorm and having that whole university experience, but the introvert in me wouldn't let me put myself through the suffering. Even though I kept referring to this place as a campus, it was really just a community college at its core. This area would be way more interesting if it were a college town, with maybe more than just two stoplights. Maybe once I blow up, I will mention how I went here and give this school some more exposure. They'd sell my books in the bookstore, let me come and give guest lectures.

"What's up, lover boy?" Joelle said, standing with AJ at the bottom of the bleachers.

"Love doesn't exist," we all said in unison. They loved to mock me.

"Whatever, bro," AJ said, wiping his face with the bottom of his shirt. "You and Brooklyn have been exchanging a lot of longing looks in the halls and in the lounge the past few days."

I ignored him and kept copying.

"And they have their last class of the day together, too," Joelle added, climbing the bleachers. "I've seen them walking each other out the school."

"We're just friends. Besides, she's not my type."

"Because she's black?" AJ said, obnoxiously loud.

"No!" I defended. "My dad is mixed, my grandpa was Italian and my Grams is black. And my mom is like Native American and something, so I'm just a Mut."

We laughed. I never had friends like this back home. Maybe it was the environment or the people. Whatever it was, I was glad to have it now.

"She's a cute girl, man, so explain," AJ prompted.

"I'm not saying she isn't hot."

"So what is it, Caleb?" Joelle and AJ continued to drill.

"It doesn't even matter anymore, because I totally told her I was uninterested yesterday."

"Oh, really?" Joelle said.

"He's bluffing," AJ added.

"I'm serious. Yesterday we were sitting in our Literary Arts class sharing a book, because she forgot hers, and that's where the conversation happened..."

"What are you doing this weekend, Caleb?" Brooklyn asked.

"You know. This and that."

They both paused and waited for more of the story.

"That's it," I concluded.

"That's you telling a girl you aren't interested?" Joelle asked.

"Yeah. I left it vague. She doesn't know what that means."

"No one knows what that means, Stevens."

"What if she thinks I was spending quality time with my lady?"

"You mean your grandma," AJ said condescendingly.

"Gross, Caleb," Joelle added.

"No, it's gross the way you two think. I just want to enjoy life." They finished my sentence with me as if 'enjoy life' was some sort of catchphrase I had. I was both annoyed and flattered by it, because I had always wanted a catchphrase.

"Whatever," AJ said, laughing as he walked off to continue to harass the girls playing ball.

"So what are you guys doing this weekend? I'm eager to like, take in the surroundings down here."

"You know… this and that," Joelle mocked me while his watch alarm went off, reminding us that we actually have classes to attend. We walked off the bleachers to go in the hallway.

"So nothing this weekend?" I persisted. AJ caught up with us at the tail end of my sentence.

"Jojo and I are skipping the rest of the day. Come!"

"Can't. Grams has her doctor visits today and I gotta be home when she's there."

"Cool. Try not to be too tied up with

your lady friend!" Joelle added, yelling
down the hall to me as they slipped out
through the side door.

I hoped Brooklyn wasn't listening to
get the wrong idea, but didn't know why.

(**KEEP STRAIGHT**)

Yesterday was pretty quiet because my
grandma was exhausted. She usually is after
her Friday appointments at the doctor. I
tried to finish a few of the short stories
I'd started writing over the past few
weeks, but I wasn't feeling motivated. At
some point I nodded off and woke up this
morning to Grams whispering to someone
downstairs. As I crept down the hall to the
top of the staircase, I saw her hand money
to a man in the doorway.

He grabbed three pill bottles out of
his pocket and I knew it had to be him, the
weed man.

I ran down the stairs before grandma
could fully shut the door.

"Hey, you piece of shit!" I yelled as
I burst through the screen door into the
lawn. "You like dealing drugs to old
ladies!"

"Excuse me?" the man said as he turned
around. I froze with confusion before I
could take another step.

My grandmother's weed man was a cop.

"I take weed from punks like you and
give it to your grandma." He took out the

money she had given him, balled it up and threw it at me. "You think five dollars would cover the amount I give her?"

"I don't know," I said, still confused.

"Yeah, you don't know shit, kid. I should arrest you for lying to a police officer."

"Seriously, I don't smoke. I wouldn't know."

"You have the right to remain silent," he said, pulling cuffs off of his belt.

"Dude! What the fuck?" was my only reaction, as this was all happening too fast for me to keep up with.

"Nooo man, I'm just messing with you," he said, laughing hysterically. "Your grandma did chemo with my mom before she passed, and ever since then I've been giving the weed I take off kids to your grandma."

"Chemo?"

"Yeah, man. Cancer's a bitch. My mom would share the weed with my grandma before their appointments. I guess you can say it's all recreational."

He said something else about arresting me if I smoked any of her supply, but it was all muffled as the word Cancer rang in my ear.

Cancer.

It's like I finally find a relationship that means something, and not

89

only is it with my grandma, it's also now
temporary? I walked back up the steps of
the porch and into the house, closing the
screen door behind me.

I turned to walk into the living room,
and there she was lighting up.

"Is everything alright, Clark?" she
asked nonchalantly.

"Grandma, you have cancer?"

"Yeah, just a little."

"What does that even mean?

"Well, it's boob cancer, and I only
have B-cups, and even then there's
shrinkage on them," she said in between
pulls while looking into the top of her
blouse at herself.

Grams reached the joint out to me and
a car honk came from outside. It was the
cop, wagging his finger 'No' at my grandma.
She laughed and slowly pulled her hand with
the joint away from me.

"Over-protective son of a gun," she
said through her teeth while still smiling
out the window. "Sweet boy, though," she
added as she took another drag followed by
a fit of coughing.

I sat down beside her and watched the
cop car pull away as she inched the joint
my way again. I shook my head no and held
up my hand. She then started with airplane
noises all around me until I finally gave
in. I wasn't a smoker or a fan of
airplanes, but given the bombshell that had

just landed on me, why not try to escape reality a bit.

I took a pull and coughed, a lot. I can't believe this is the first time I've ever smoked weed, and it is with my grandma. I took a few more and then handed it back to her. We sat in silence, staring out the window while the elephant in the room sat between us.

"So that's why you smoke? Because it helps with the nausea of chemo?"

"Oh no. I've smoked long before I knew I had boob cancer." She laughed and coughed out a cloud of smoke before she continued, "but I guess now you can stop giving me mess for smoking now."

"Grandma, don't call it boob cancer. That makes it weird for me. Just say breast cancer, or BC."

"I'll refer to my tits anyway I please."

"Jeez, Grams," I said, creeped out. I handed her back the weed and stood up. "Do my parents know?" I asked. I don't know what answer I was expecting her to give me, but I wasn't expecting the response I got back.

"I told them. Yeah. I told them when I found out a year and a half ago, but they didn't think anything of it. They were like, 'Well, you are seventy-two, so your expiration is past due.' I can tell they think I am just being dramatic, so they send money blindly so I can pay for whatever I need to as long as it keeps me from calling them and complaining."

I think that was the first time I heard this emotion in my grandmother's voice. It sounded like pain, which triggered with the weed made me tear up a little. I didn't know what to say.

"Grams."

"Don't," she said, cutting me off. She knew I was stalling. She knew me better than I knew myself. "People have died from less."

"I guess," was all the answer I could muster up. Grams looked at me and laughed.

"Gotta learn to say more than that when a girl is pouring her heart out to you."

"I love you," I laughed. "You know that."

"Just like a man to use 'I love you' as a pacifier." But she laughed, too.

"Just like a woman to say 'I love you too' without saying it at all." I got up and kissed her on the forehead.

"Right answers, babe. You'll be fine."

CHAPTER NINE

(**90mi**)

"Oh no. What's wrong, Caleb?"

"Why do you assume something is wrong because I called you, mom?"

"You never call your mother, or me for that matter."

"Dad? What are you guys doing together?" Neither of them answered right away. They probably didn't know why themselves.

"We are hanging out, becoming friends all over again," my mom said, finally breaking the silence. "I'm so glad you called me, honey."

"Yeah, champ, your absence made us realize that besides all the history, good and bad, we still have one thing in common; that we love you."

I felt instantly enraged. I mean, I can't remember the last time my parents told me they genuinely loved me, and now when I do hear it, it's being used an excuse that will just backfire on them later.

I'm not even sure it's rage I'm

feeling. Maybe this emotion consuming me is jealousy.

"To what do we owe the pleasure?" my mother asked.

"Just wanted to say hi," I stalled. They were silent, but I was well-versed in this tactic from being with Grams. Grams is famous for leaving blank spaces in conversations. They bait the person who's talking to keep talking and fill in the void. Perks from her days as a therapist, I assumed.

"How's classes?" dad broke first. I could hear him grimace soon after, and I assume my mom had kicked him under the table.

"Fine."

"Yeah?" he continued.

"Yeah. I've reached back out to a program that sent a letter a while ago about my future with them. I just have to get some additional docs they asked for."

"Champ, that's great to hear!"

"Good, baby. Good."

I could tell they were gearing up to go off on a tangent. I was too broken to care, so I just blurted out the first thing that came to mind.

"I miss her," I mumbled.

"What was that, son? Speak up. I couldn't hear you," my dad prompted me.

"I said I miss Brooklyn." I trembled at the sound of the phrase.

"Well, when you come back to visit again we can go to Brooklyn and eat at your favorite place."

"No, mom, I miss Brooklyn!" I said, voice cracking from holding in tears.

"*I miss the way she laughed.*

I miss the way she used to finish my sentences.

I miss how she always wore the same perfume, but smelled different whenever her mood changed.

I miss how she was always covered in paint from her work.

I miss the way her eyes and skin would shine like golden cinnamon when the sun hit.

I miss the way her nipples would always poke through her shirt because she hated weari—"

"Caleb!" my mother interrupted.

"Sorry, champ. All we heard was nipples," my dad said, dismissing the very rare moment of me opening up to them. "You just need to get out more."

"He's probably locked himself in that old room of yours, filming. Hasn't been to any of those classic house parties your father used to drag me to," my mom added.

"Wrong. I've been going out. I've been to-"

"Oh yeah?" she challenged.

"Yeah," I defended. I listened to them forget I was even present and start

95

reminiscing on a few of those parties.

"Hello?" I continued, "This isn't about any of that. It's about Brooklyn."

"Speaking of Brooklyn, we are trying to order food here at that sushi spot in Williamsbu—"

I hung up. I don't know what I thought calling my mom would do for my mood, but it didn't help. I just hated sitting in this hospital helplessly.

The beeping from different machines, the constant cold air as if they were trying to preserve the old people before they expired, the smell of left out hospital food, not knowing when your loved one was leaving the hospital or if they ever would. It's all very depressing. Trying to get an update from my grandmother's doctors was impossible.

My mom texted me:

'Sorry, honey. When your grandma pulls through there is a place in Brooklyn we can put her.'

It amazed me how quick they were to throw her in a home, and not even ask how she was doing. I started to distrust my own emotions. Was it the fact she was saying 'We' in reference to her and Dad? When 'We' didn't work before, the family moved forward with just being individually 'Us.'

I started to picture a version of my family in red jumpsuits and holding golden scissors. I'd be willing to trade pleases, no problem.

I pulled up a chair to the doorway of grandma's room as I whistled *I Got 5 on It* from that Jordan Peele movie. I couldn't see her like this. I want to keep that image of a short, round, happy, brittle but strong-willed woman. I don't think my will is strong enough at this point to see her like this. To see the person who has been more than just motivation, but my reason to—

"Clark?" she called out, interrupting my thought.

"Yeah, grandma?"

"Just making sure you were still over there."

"Yes ma'am. Why, what's wrong?" I walked into the room in a panic. She had the towel over her face because she didn't want me freaking out. She knew me all too well. "You don't have to do that, grandma."

"And risk you passing out and getting a bed next to me? I don't want to hear you snore all day." She laughed.

"I don't sno—"

"Where's that nice girl you used to be with?" she said, cutting me off.

"Not sure."

"Well, go find her," she said through a fit of coughs.

"Are you okay?"

"Of course," she said. Her voice was muffled into the towel she was using to

97

cover her mouth, struggling to catch her breath. I ran out of the room to call for a nurse.

"I'm fine, Caleb," she said, starting to cough again. I knew she was serious because she called me by my actual name. Machines started to beep and alarms rang from her bed that summoned doctors and nurses before I could even react. I walked down the hall and sat on the windowsill a few doors down from her room. I could hear them fussing and bickering in there until finally the staff exited one by one.

"Um, excuse me, is she okay?" I said, chasing down the group of orderlies.

"She's fine. She pulled something out of her arm trying to adjust herself in her bed. She wanted our attention anyway for some extra Jell-O."

"Christ, I'm sorry."

"No worries. She's a strong woman," the nurse said, putting her hand on my shoulder to comfort me.

This nurse's name was Victoria, and she was the sweetest of all the staff that actually cared about their patients. I walked back in my grandmother's room to her smiling and eating a cup of Jell-O. She started to cough, trying to contain her chuckle while attempting to ignore I was glaring at her. Finally she burst into a full-on laughing coughing fit again.

I took the empty cup and pulled the

blanket up on her some more. She turned over with a smile and started to fall back asleep.

This isn't how I had planned on spending my weekend.

I was starving. I checked my account and was surprised to see three hundred extra dollars. I had been doing a bunch of reviews lately for that blog, and I guess I had forgotten that I got paid for them. I ordered a pizza from the local Italian place and started scrolling through my camera roll.

One of my favorite things to do was to pour sad music on an already sad mood like gasoline on a fire. I started scrolling through my Spotify when I noticed new songs added to the playlist Brooklyn and I had shared. I wondered if she had been feeling some of the same things that I did.

I opened my messages and went to her text thread. I started to type a simple 'hey' and watched the cursor blink in and out, as if it were taunting me.

I backed out and erased the entire thread. I closed Spotify and went to my actual music library and let my 'Sadderday & Slumpday' playlist drift me down a dark, melancholy stream. If only it had started raining, it would be the happy start to a sad weekend.

A knock at the door from a nurse brought me back to reality. She was a beautiful Indian woman I had seen on the floor. I actually think Grams tried telling me about her a few times, but we had never crossed paths.

"Hi. I'm sorry. Is everything okay?"

"Yeah, why wouldn't they be?" my grandma answered.

"I just heard crying and wanted to check and see if you needed me, ma'am."

"Yeah," I said, quickly sitting up straight. "I think that was from the room next to ours. I heard it too." I pointed to the wall next to me.

"That wall faces a storage closet," she said. My Grandma looked at me in disappointment.

Another knock came at the door. It was the pizza man saving me from the moment.

"Sonya, honey, have a slice of whatever my very single grandson ordered."

"Thank you, but I just ate and have other patients to check on. It was nice meeting you," she said before leaving the room. I took the pizza box and placed it on the bed. I handed Grams a slice.

"Didn't even introduce yourself," she said, shaking her head at me.

"I didn't know what to say."

"Because you were too busy crying."

"At max it was a whimper," I defended immediately.

"I only asked about Brooklyn earlier because of her brownies. You are so much

more focused on work now than I've ever
seen you. Even if most of your reviews are
on silly chick flicks."

"Thanks, Grams. I'm just trying to get
into this Sundance program. I missed my
window on positions, but if I'm persistent,
who knows."

"You'll get some good news soon," she
said, slurping up a piece of stringy
cheese. My personal Oracle.

CHAPTER TEN

My phone rang. It was an unsaved number, but I didn't feel like talking so I left it on the arm of the chair. Grams usually was sleepy and lethargic after her doctor visits, but now that I knew it was cancer it just made me crazy.

I was consumed by what that stupid cop had told me earlier today. And, because of stupid doctor-patient confidentiality, I didn't have any information besides what she gave me.

To do something, I'd been cleaning like crazy. Since the windows were usually open, tons of pollen blew into the house. I told myself that if I cleaned it up and gave Grams some clean air to breathe, it would help. I brought an air humidifier, extra pillows for her chair, and was driving her crazy with questions.

Grams had gotten into this Marie Kondo woman on Netflix, so she'd been using my mania to her advantage and had me folding and throwing out everything. Gram's plan backfired, though, when I kept handing her things to see if it sparked joy. I was driving her crazy, too. I just wanted to somehow make up for the time I hadn't been here.

I sat by her while she pretended to sleep so I would stop bothering her.

"Your Grace," I whispered in my medieval *Game of Thrones* accent. A grin flashed quickly across her face, exposing her horrible sleep charade. I cleared my throat, letting her know she wasn't fooling me.

"Blimey, you are a bloody pain in me arse, caretaker," she blurted out in a laugh.

"I win."

"How? Australian accent."

"Nope, it wasn't," I laughed back. "You hungry? I was thinking of maybe going to this sandwich place Brooklyn was telling me about."

"And who's this Brooklyn?"

"Nobody."

"God forbid it's a nice young lady," she said as I helped her up off the sofa. We walked over to her chair.

"Yeah, God forbid," I laughed.

"After you take me to church today, you need to get out of the house. You are driving me crazy," she instructed. Grandma's idea of church was watching some preacher on TV. I went into the kitchen and got some stuff to make her a sandwich while she watched TV. Out of nowhere, I heard my grandma talking to someone. I assumed Officer Robin Hood had got some more weed to give her. When I walked back into the living room, I saw that she was on my phone.

"Okay, honey, he'll be there."

"GRANDMA?"

"Okay, honey, hope to meet you soon as well." Before I could snatch the phone away, the conversation was over.

"Grandma." I paused. "Who did you just call?"

"I called back that Brooklyn girl, such a sweet name. She said something about a party and I told her you would be there."

"Grams!" I complained as she laughed. She grabbed her lighter and a joint from her ashtray and lit it. She took a pull or two and handed it to me.

"Here," she said with a smile.

Before I knew it, I was standing in front of what felt like a deleted scene from that *Project X* movie.

"The party animal has arrived!" AJ yelled as he walked by as the caboose for a passing Congo-line. I made my way through the maze of red solo cups in the kitchen to the back door, which had been recently torn off one of the hinges. I stepped out onto the back porch to see there were fifty to sixty people in the back yard talking, dancing, revving truck engines, and playing horseshoes and touch strip football.

"I can't believe I am at a party where people are playing horseshoes," I said out loud.

"Is that the only thing that bothers you, city boy?" I turned around and saw Brooklyn handing me a cup. The way we kept running into each other almost felt scripted.

"It's like I'm stuck in the twilight zone," I answered while I took a sip out of the cup. "This is amazing. What's in this?"

"Kool-Aid," she said, laughing at how impressed I was with the drink.

"Oh nooo! Who owns this house, Pastor Jim Jones?"

"No, Deacon Juelz does."

"That's not the reference I was trying to make. See, James Jon—"

"Relax," she interrupted me. "I got the joke." She laughed. Sometimes I hated my own humor, regardless of how much I amused myself. "I love that autumn crisp in the air. Some people argue spring is the beginning of the year, but I think it's fall," she said.

"How so?"

"I don't really have an astrological explanation. More just my own opinion."

"Noted," I laughed.

"What are the parties like in Jersey? I imagine a bunch of spray tans, hair gel, and people screaming DTF."

"You must have watched too much *Jersey Shore*. Besides, you can't just call me a city boy. You aren't from here, either." We walked off the back porch through the crowd of people.

"I'm an army brat. So no, I'm not a country girl or city girl, more of a nomad. I can't really say I even know who I am, sometimes. I moved a lot as a kid, and right after I had made real friends, we would have to pack up and move again. I've lived in Fort Leavenworth, Kansas; Fort Bliss, Texas; Washington… oh, Fort Shafter, Hawaii—"

"Hawaii?" I interrupted.

"Yeah. Hawaii."

"That's pretty awesome to say."

"I guess. I mean, I've lived so many places I don't even know where I'm from. Sometimes we'd return to the same base and I'd get to go to the same schools, but eventually my dad thought it would be best if I was homeschooled, so it stopped mattering."

"Well, people suck, so who needs them."

"Yeah, I agree. But so much moving made it hard to find love even though my dad says I'm gonna be a man-eater like my mom—aaannd I'm rambling. Sorry. I'm a sharer when I'm drunk."

"No, it's fine. Continue," I insisted, but she refused. We walked a little in awkward silence until it wasn't awkward anymore. It was that good silence. That 'we don't have to talk, we can just enjoy each other's company' silence. After our third or fourth lap around the house, we climbed a tree and sat and laughed at everyone at the party. Usually at parties that was my favorite solitary pastime, but it was nice having company.

"So what are you going to school for?" she asked, changing the course of the mood.

"Well, I've been applying to this place in L.A."

"Nice! I love Cali," she interrupted.

"No, I meant Louisiana," I said with as much confidence as I could. She laughed hysterically. "Can I finish my story?" I giggled, half-embarrassed.

"Sorry, sorry, yes, please finish. So you are moving to L.A," she said, smiling. We talked about how I was going to take my 'Plan B' dream job as a film critic in L.A. over my real actual 'Plan A' dream job to be a screenwriter. She listened to me rant about how I'd love to take the opportunity I found for a romantic comedy web series screenwriter, but I was just afraid it wouldn't work out. She poked fun of my beliefs of love 'being a fairy tale,' but I held my ground.

We debated and talked about the jobs for what seemed like hours in that tree. The party was all background noise and the only thing that existed in that moment was us. She encouraged me with so much passion and determination to go after my dreams.

Live life. Don't let it live you.

Get out of your comfort zone.

Believe in everything that they tell you not to.

All the quotes you would see on aesthetically pleasing Tumblr posts. Maybe it was the buzz I had, but I started to read more into what she was saying than she probably intended. I thought I was right when she grabbed my hand, but then after she vomited ten feet below us I realized she was just bracing herself as much as she could.

Our moment was interrupted. Cop sirens and spotlights sent a stampede of the minors in attendance into a panic. We jumped out of the tree, missing the vomit puddle by inches. Brooklyn took my hand as we ran into the woods. I instantly started to freak out and thought of how I could have stumbled into an M. Night Shyamalan movie. I think I was still a little high.

"Um, I can't go any further," I said while jerking my arm away from her grip and stopping in my tracks. "I'd rather go to jail than get lost and eaten by a witch."

Brooklyn stared at me in disbelief.

"Relax. The road's literally right there."

I guess I was overreacting. I could

see the yellow line in the middle of the road from where we were in the woods. She pushed me down into the grass and fell on top of me as a car slowly drove towards us with a light shining in the bushes, looking for something or someone.

"Brooklyn, it's the cops. We have to run."

She covered my mouth, muffling my plea.

"They want us to run," she whispered. "Just relax, Caleb." The car slowly drove by us as the spotlight missed us by inches.

"Why are you looking for something that doesn't exist?" I whispered to her.

"What did I say I was looking for?" she asked while looking down at me.

"Love," I replied. The awkward silence was back again as she looked into my eyes with confusion. I would have kissed her if her breath hadn't smelled of sauerkraut and red Kool-Aid from vomiting. She crawled off me and helped me up out of the mud.

"Finding love is possible."

"Yeah, so is hitting the lottery."

"Hitting the lottery is still possible. A win is a win. It may not be the amount you wanted, but probably the amount you didn't know you needed," she added. I hated that she had a point. "I've always felt like love is a place where you can always feel at home. And I guess I'm just looking for that feeling."

"Sounds like you want some grandiose romance novel situation, with a castle and unicorn," I taunted.

"Maybe it sounds grand to you, but I think it's obtainable."

"Sounds like a fairytale."

"Your point?"

"They aren't real."

"Even if that were true, and it isn't, fantasizing about being treated like royalty is okay with me. I'm a sucker for a good horror story," she laughed.

"You are crazy," I laughed with her.

"Well, you kinda have to be to believe in love. To use your phrase, It's the only socially accepted version of crazy, besides Kanye."

We walked back to the house to investigate the aftermath of the bust. Her words lingered in the air like they were taunting me—or rather my views. One wrong move can turn a fairy tale into a horror story. Imagine if the prince had slipped climbing up Rapunzel's hair, and look at Romeo and Juliet.

I wish my brain didn't work the way it did sometimes, but it does. At least this time I could sit on my words.

"Kings County," I said under my breath.

"What was that?"

"You said royalty, and it made me think of Kings County. Brooklyn's real name, I guess. I mean, people hear the name Brooklyn and think high rents, Hipsters, Biggie and Jay-Z, but just from our first real conversation, I can tell you—" I cut myself off.

"No, come on, Caleb. Please?" she begged, taking my hands in hers.

"I don't know. I guess, just like the borough, I can tell there's more to you once you get to know it."

"You must really like Brooklyn." She smiled menacingly.

"I think growing up in Jersey and then finally becoming the age to go out to different places on your own in the city, you discover these entirely new worlds just a few train stops away."

"Kinda like people that live at the beach, they hardly ever go," she added.

"Yeah. You appreciate it more."

"Well, hopefully you will tell me more about Brooklyn, and I will finally be able to get to know myself."

"I'd like that." We finally got back to the yard where the last few bits of people were starting to leave. I wasn't sure what that conversation was, but it was something. Something that made my spidey sense tingle.

"Good," she said, before she ran off to knock on a window of a car. The door opened and she was greeted by what seemed to be a hundred girl giggles and screams.

She jumped in and left me standing at the mailbox. I watched her pull away, and I could swear I could hear "I Don't Want to Wait" by Paula Cole.

"STEEEEVENS!" someone yelled from an upstairs window. Only one person called me that. AJ. "Did you have sex with her?"

"What?" I was singing the lyrics to Dawson's Creek theme song to myself and lost in my own world.

"I SAID DID YOU HAVE SEX WITH HER!" AJ yelled louder.

"NO! Dude, quit yelling!" A neighbor's light from next door came on and an old man pulled back the curtains.

"Dude, I couldn't hear what you said!" AJ yelled again. I looked back at the neighbor, and he was on the phone. I'm guessing he was calling the cops, and that he was the culprit who called in the first place.

"The cops are coming back, man! I'm gonna go!" I warned.

"No, dude, you're a ho!" he replied, laughing hysterically.

I walked over to my bike, texted him that I thought the cops were coming, and left.

I walked into the house. My grandma was knocked out snoring in her chair with some sort of infomercial on. I tried to creep past and not wake her, which was easy for me because I felt like I was hovering in mid-air.

"I'm not sleeping, just resting my eyes."

"That's called sleep, grandma," I replied while hovering back down a few steps.

"How was the party, Clark?" she said mischievously.

I leaned on the doorframe to the living room and smiled at her.

"Eh, it was alright."

"Well, did you have sex with her?"

"Uh, excuse me?"

"I said, 'Well good, help me up.'"

Either my mind was playing tricks on me or she was. I walked over and bent down so she could grab onto me to help steady herself. We started walking to her bedroom so she could get some more rest.

"You must have had a good time. It's past midnight," she lectured.

"I just took my time coming back home is all."

"Well, you have that same look on your face your father did when he met your mother—"

"No thanks, grandma," I interrupted. "I know that relationships are just an excuse for people to use because they hate the thought of being their own company. Because they suck."

"Lie to yourself all you want, Clark,

but you can't lie to me," she said,
laughing. She shook me loose to go into the
bathroom.

Had I been lying to myself? Maybe
Grams is the Oracle. But does that make me
the One? I walked back down the hall to
head upstairs to my room. I looked out the
blinds onto the porch as if I expected
Brooklyn to be standing there like some 90s
movie. Before I reached the stairs, though,
the toilet flushed and the door swung open
down the hall.

"You are gonna fall in love with that
girl, Caleb. Could just be temporarily, or
even at the wrong time." She paused to
cough and I smelled weed smoke. "Maybe it
will be forever, or maybe even too late,
but you will fall in love," she said while
walking in her bedroom.

"Don't fall asleep with that thing lit
in there!" I yelled. She laughed and
coughed as she closed her door and turned
on the radio. She couldn't sleep without
the radio.

I turned and walked upstairs to my
room, repeating to myself what she had
said.

Maybe...

CHAPTER ELEVEN

"Fam, who parties that hard on a Monday? The culture here is amazing. Our parties were way different back in Jersey," I said, grabbing the other end of the beer keg.

"Bro, it's Friday. We are on to the next one."

"Well, duh, JoJo. He's hyped because they can't have house parties up there. It's only apartments," AJ joked.

We walked out of the cooler into the gas station where Joelle was waiting with the other keg. AJ and Joelle had found their names in some sort of underground party-planning circuit. Other colleges had heard about the last party these guys threw, and now their reputations were like A-list celebrities in the surrounding counties.

AJ paid for the beer, then grabbed one handle of each of the kegs while Joelle and I grabbed the empty ends. We shuffled the kegs out of the door. I forget sometimes, with all his jokes and carefree attitude, how strong AJ actually was. It seemed he was the actual brains behind this idea.

"Alright, cool," Joelle said, half-dying from the short walk outside to his car. "We gotta get back to campus to get you to the bus for your game. Caleb, are you still gonna help me with sneaking these bad boys into dry county this evening?"

"Shit!" I exclaimed.

"Stevens," AJ said, disappointed.

"No, I totally forgot, but it's fine. I'll be there."

"You sure, bro? If not I can just wait on AJ and do it the day of the party."

"No, it's fine. I was just gonna study with Brooklyn, but the test isn't for a while, so it's cool."

"Whatever, let's go! Drive and talk, drive and talk," AJ said, slamming the door impatiently. He opened it again and clapped his hands together in prayer style. "Dude, I'm so sorry," he laughed, "we just need to go."

"I'm gonna like ban you from closing my car doors forever, bro," Joelle said, making sure AJ closed the door gently the second time. As we drove back to the school, I tried to figure out what I could tell Brooklyn to break our date.

Not that it was a date, but it was something.

"Dude," Joelle said, elbowing me.

"What's up?"

"It's cool if you wanna try getting closer to Brooklyn, bro. Like everybody knows you like her."

"Fam. Back in Jersey, you are a sucker if you bail on your boys for a chick. It's cool, she'll get the hint."

"Caleb. Stop," Joelle said, annoyed.

"No, seriously," I laughed.

"No, dude, when I say stop I mean like enough. This isn't Jersey."

"Yeah, Stevens," AJ agreed with Joelle. "Besides, if you stand up Brooklyn, she may tap into her dad's sleeper cell soldier genes and kill you."

"Yeah, and then you'll wish you were in Jersey," Joelle added to AJ's randomness. We laughed.

I guess they were right. I mean, if this were Jersey I wouldn't even have gone to that party. Partly because it would have been hell trying to get a text back on a group chat about it.

With that thought, I decided to open my Facebook messenger and peek in on the group chat. It was a collective of maybe six or seven homies and a few dudes whose names I knew, but didn't know them. I forgot I had muted the chat and saw that it was as active as ever. I looked for anyone asking how I was, or any message directly to me, but only scrolled through some funny memes about *Rick and Morty* and saved them to show Brooklyn later.

117

That's when I remembered I still had to do something about my other commitment.

With a stroke of luck, a text from Brooklyn came through: *Hey I don't feel like studying today. Some other time?*

Part of me wished I could have canceled before she did. Then I couldn't figure out why I had that thought at all. Why was this girl so mesmerizing to me? In Jersey this never happened. Of course, there's an exception to the rule, but those girls were from Manhattan. I missed cutting class with the homies to go and just cause chaos as a collective, even if I was mostly just a bystander and I usually broke away to do my own thing. I guess that's the same sort of role I've found myself in here, too. Big difference is, I feel included, or maybe depended on. It feels more genuine.

Joelle pulled into the parking lot and AJ jumped out of the car before Joelle could fully stop it. I couldn't hold in my laugh because I knew AJ did it purposely to set him off. I climbed over the center console into the back seat to close AJ's door and could sense Joelle's heart jump out of his chest when my feet touched his seats.

Joelle pulled around the lot and stopped at the stop sign before turning on the road.

"To Brooklyn's?"

"Nah, dude. She's out back. I'm with

my brother tonight," I said, adding some sauce to it to try and sound cool.

"Cool. So she canceled on you," he laughed.

"Yup," I came clean, joining him in laughing. "What gave it away?"

"The sauce."

"Damn it. I knew it." We continued laughing.

Joelle was on a throwback kick this week, and we had gotten lost in the playlist Siri was playing at random. Joelle considered himself some sort of purist. He had a first-generation iPod that had songs with tags from LimeWire on them still. This was his form of vinyl record collecting. Drake's song "From Time" featuring Jhene Aiko came on and the car turned into a karaoke session.

"So, bro," I said awkwardly. "Hillary."

"Yeah?" he laughed.

"Gonna get married and all that?" I asked. He didn't answer immediately. He seemed to really think on the answer. Or maybe he was wondering why I was asking.

"If I'm lucky," he said finally.

"Dope," I said, leaving a weird pause in the air. Before it matured into an awkward silence, I asked another question. "When?"

"Huh?"

"Like you have an idea for popping the

119

question and stuff?" I probed.

"Nah, man, I don't," he laughed. "You got marriage on the brain? Think she's the one?"

"I am never getting married, bro."

"Why not?"

"I thought I had found this girl who was the one but, long story short, she got married."

Joelle sat quiet for a bit. It was clear there was a lot more to be said on that subject, I just didn't feel like saying it. I tried to play it off and played with the iPod, cycling through songs. After a few more miles we pulled over to the side of the road.

I thought he was being a bit dramatic at first.

"Dude, it's not that serious. She just wasn't the one. Not that big of a deal," I defended, looking in his direction.

"Dude, shut up," he said, scrolling through his phone. "They bailed."

"Who bailed?"

"The kids buying the alcohol."

"Kids as in kids, kids?"

"No. I mean, not like elementary school kids. Like high schoolers, maybe, not our problem," Joelle said, busting a U-turn. "I wonder what Escobar would do when his buyers flaked," he mumbled to himself.

"Murder, I think," I responded.

"It's hard out here for suppliers. You

120

know nothing about the business," Joelle said in a horrible attempt of a Spanish accent.

"*You* don't even know anything about the business. It's probably more money throwing the parties yourselves instead of just supplying the alcohol and charging a few bucks more than you did for the keg."

Joelle listed to my proposal as if he was really calculating my words.

"I'll speak it over with my partner," he said, attempting the accent again.

We played some Big Pun songs, which I thought was problematic, considering, but it just turned out to be a throwback playlist. On the way back I told him he could drop me off at the campus because I had left my house keys in the lounge.

Suddenly, Joelle reached over and picked up the iPod. He paused the music.

"We can talk about it if you want," Joelle said out of the blue.

"About what?"

It took a while for him to get the answer out there. "The engaged girl," he said finally. "Seemed like it really hit home there for you—"

"Noooo!" I laughed awkwardly, trying to drown out what he was saying. "It's nothing. Wasn't traumatic or anything."

"You sure?"

"Yeah. It's straight."

Joelle looked at me. Analyzing me.

"It's straight," I said again, laughing. He turned the music back on and we continued the drive. When we got back to the school, I jumped out before the car had fully stopped, imitating AJ but not as smoothly. I was waiting for Joelle to yell and curse at me. When he didn't, I turned to see him standing in front of the swinging car door I had left open.

"Dude, we aren't done talking about that girl, Caleb," he persisted.

"Fine, fine," I gave in. "When I come back out."

"Nah, Mister Left My Door Open," he laughed while giving me the middle finger. He pulled away and left me.

Walking through the school, it was a lot quieter than during the day. I went into the lounge to ask the cashiers if any keys had been turned in, but none had.

What I did find in return though, was Brooklyn. She was sitting with her back to the doorway, so she didn't see me standing there. She seemed to be either focused or spaced out, it was hard to tell. I tried to sneak away before she saw me, but I wasn't the most graceful, bumping into a table and knocking over an empty tray that was left there.

"Caleb?" she said, turning in her seat and looking at me.

"Oh. I didn't see you there. Must have walked right by you."

"Yeah, must have. What are you doing here?"

"Lost my keys."

"These keys?" She said, pulling my house keys from inside her overalls. "They were on the floor, Caleb."

"Damn. Lucky me you found them." I reached out my hand for the keys, and she dropped them back into whatever compartment had been keeping them.

"Why were you creeping out of here?" she asked suspiciously.

"You texted and said you didn't want to study, then I saw you here and figured if you were studying alone you must not have wanted to see me."

"Does it look like I am studying?" she said, holding out her arms in an odd pose. I laughed and looked at her. Her arms and clothes were covered in splashes of white, red and pink paint. Her denim overalls looked older than the both of us combined. Underneath was a white sports bra that looked like she had drawn a pink heart on it with her finger not too long ago. Her hair was tied back with a scarf like an incredibly cute babushka.

"*Bizarre Adventure*?" I asked.

"No, Ginyu Force," she said impressed. "Such a classic reference," she commended me.

"Thank you. Though I've never watched that JoJo show."

"I take back my admiration," she said, offended.

I went to get some food before the cooks left for the night. The women there were nice enough to give me the "not too old" food for free, and I was able to nab a chocolate milk. Not sure if it would have been nicer if they just had made me something, but a blessing is a blessing. I walked back over to the table and saw Brooklyn spaced out again.

"What's with the face?" I asked as I sat.

"It's this Pandora station they have in here. It sucks, but every once in a while at night they play some songs that remind me of my mom. She was a photographer and these were her lucky overalls. I come here to paint in Valspar's class because she has all the shit I need to express myself."

"Painting is the only way you express yourself?"

"The only time I can really get anyone to see where I'm coming from is if I paint it. I know, I'm a loser."

"Not at all, maybe when you were in high school but not now."

"Oh really?" She laughed, "What were you like in high school?"

"Well, if I wasn't hanging out with Lauren and Brody down at Laguna, I was probably hitting on teachers with Pacey down at the video store we worked at. Sometimes I'd hang out with Franco and Rogen to pick on the geeks and freaks, to hide the fact I was indeed both in my alone time. And if I didn't want to be a geek alone I would hang out with the Leery kid over analyzing Spielberg movies until Joey came over."

Brooklyn stared at me with an admiring glare. "What?" I laughed.

"Oh nothing. I was waiting for you to say '*Well if it was Friday I would be with Smokey and Craig*, Or *Dueling with your boy Yugi*." She said condenscendingly while she imitated my voice. We laughed. I was impressed how quickly she caught on to my nerdy response. "Probably a very sexless life." She added.

"Saddly." I laughed, throwing my hands in the air.

"Liar." She smiled shoving me in the shoulder. "Speaking of which, where are Hillary's boyfriend and the human jockstrap?" She continued.

"No idea. Guess it's just us tonight."

"Cool," she said, eating fries off my tray. "You don't mind?"

"Mind what? That it's just us? Of course not."

"I meant me eating your fries, Caleb."

"I knew that." I didn't know that. "The fries were the only thing that was good, but they're cold now. The food here sucks like prison food."

"And because you've been to prison you'd know," she said sarcastically.

"They called me Khal Drogo in the pen," I said in my best *Game of Thrones* voice. I sounded dumb, like if Jason Statham and Seth Rogen had a baby, but Brooklyn died laughing anyway.

"So if you were home, what would you eat?"

"Probably whatever was left over in my fridge. Tailored ham or-"

"No," she laughed, "I meant Jersey."

"Awh, man, where I got off the Path train sometimes there'd be a stand with an Italian Hot Dog I'd kill for."

"A hot dog?"

"This isn't just any hot dog. It's a deep-fried frank and deep-fried potatoes with peppers and onions all on Italian bread."

"So the bread makes it Italian," she said while laughing.

"You're not worthy."

"No, no, no, it sounds good, it really does."

"It is good, man. Topped off with ketchup and it's perfect."

"You lost me at ketchup. Gross."

"What? You don't like ketchup?"

"Communists like ketchup."

"Brooklyn, I just saw you take the tomato off my burger and eat it first. But you don't like ketchup?"

"Two separate things."

"Whatever. If I was in Brooklyn, I would probably just get a sandwich from a corner store."

"What? That sounds even less appealing."

"Holy shit," I said in shock. "You've never had a bodega sandwich. They aren't specific to just Brooklyn, but I made it my business to only eat them from Brooklyn. You walk in and you're surrounded by whatever Spanish music is playing, usually a cat or two, and an older gentleman in the corner kinda just talking to whoever walks in, possibly the owner. Then you go up to the glass case where all the Boars Head meats and cheeses are and place your order."

Brooklyn stared with a confused smile on her face. "Bodega sandwich?" she said.

"A bodega sandwich. Oh, and every guy fixing the sandwich you just call Papi."

"Can I make a bodega sandwich?"

"Bfff, you'd have better luck making the Italian hot dog." She laughed again. It was nice to be enjoyed or thought of as funny. "What about you? What would you be eating if we weren't locked away in school right now?"

"I'm a picky eater, but it also depends which way the wind blows, and then I could eat really anything."

"The complexities of the female mind."

"I definitely wouldn't be drinking milk with all that food in front of you. You are gonna get sick."

"Well," I said, taking a bite of stale fries, "good thing you are here to take care of me." I finished by purposely slurping up the rest of the milk in my container.

She nudged me on the shoulder and we laughed some more. I think she liked my laugh, because when I laughed, she laughed even harder. We decided to follow each other on Spotify and then judge each other on the music the other listened to. Before I knew it, hours had passed, and we left the lounge with a joint playlist of five hundred songs. I couldn't have hoped for a better night.

CHAPTER TWELVE
(**500mi**)

Brooklyn and I ran into the grocery store from the unexpected rainfall outside. She had refused to share my umbrella with me, so she was soaked. I shook the umbrella dry through the doors and stepped back inside. I took off my coat and put it around her, and she grimaced when I touched her.

"Do you know what you want to get to eat?" I asked her while she grabbed a cart from the rack.

"Not really," she said while walking away.

"Well, we can just get a basket to carry so we don't have to push the cart around."

She didn't answer, and instead just let go of the cart and walked down an aisle. I snatched a basket and ran to catch up with her.

"So, what are you getting?" she asked.

"Oh yeah, leave it up to me so you can disagree," I said jokingly. We were walking down the baking aisle, so I grabbed a box of brownie mix off the shelf.

"How about we bake, babe?"

"No. I'm not in the mood to bake."

I walked up to her to take her hand to
hold, but she moved it. I watched her walk
down the aisle away from me.

I can tell something was wrong, but I
don't know what it is.

(**REROUTING**)

(**912 Miles to Destination**)

"So Brooklyn, why are we here again?"
I asked while pushing a cart and nearly
knocking over a display of on sale drinks.
My alarm went off on an old digital watch I
had found in my dad's room. 2:13.

"Running late for something?" Brooklyn
said at me checking my watch.

"If I said yes, would that reveal why
we are here?" I laughed.

"No."

"And what about that piece I wanted to
write up?"

"You can do that later. Fine. If you
are going to ask a hundred questions, we
are here because I want something to snack
on."

"But you said you weren't hungry."

"Correct."

"But hungry enough to snack."

She turned to look at me with a death
glare. "Also correct, Caleb."

I looked down at our cart. It was

filled with chips, soda, cookies, milk and ice cream.

"I can hear you silently judging me, love," she said in a fake English accent.

"No, mate. Me? Never."

"That's Australian, Caleb," she said, breaking character as she ran around the corner at top speed. I followed her around the corner to find her holding an armful of brownie mix.

"Okay, that's it, Brooklyn. We already have a cart full of—"

"Shhhhhhhh, Caleb," she said while pouring all the boxes into my arms. "Leave the cart."

"What?"

"Leave the cart. The bagger I despise is working today and he has to put this stuff back. So leave it."

I've become an accessory to crime, I thought while we walked up front to the registers.

"You said you wanted to do something to make a good first impression on my grandma?" I asked when I finally caught up with her in line.

"Correct again. Wow, Caleb, I'll have to figure out a nice prize for you."

"So you are gonna make her brownies?"

Brooklyn reached across the register to where the cashier was and grabbed the microphone.

"Ladies and Gentlemen, boys and girls,

131

we have a winnerrrr!"

"What are you doing?" I laughed, a little shocked.

"Sir, what is your name?" She held the mic towards me to speak. I shook my head no. "Caleb, that's a sexy name, Caleb," she continued. "You answered all four questions right in a rooooowwww!"

I looked around at the three people in the store, shooting down my hopes that it was a ghost town at the moment. The door behind the service desk opened and a woman in a buttoned-up blouse and manager nametag walked over to us.

My heart sank. The typical Jersey kid in me wanted to snatch the food we had and just run out of the store. I didn't act on that impulse, though. I felt Brooklyn and I had ended up playing some sort of game of chicken, and I wanted to see how it would play out.

The woman grabbed the mic from Brooklyn to speak into it. I assumed the charade to be over and looked over at Brooklyn, but she didn't look shaken.

I expected the woman to speak an apology to the customers in the store or a cover-up for her-off-the-clock employee's disruption. The woman looked at me with a scowl, and then smiled mischievously at Brooklyn.

"I'm gonna go ahead and go, guys," I surrendered, swerving out of the way of the

Mack Truck Brooklyn was speeding towards me.

"You can't go," the women said. "Not without your prize! Brooklyn, what did he win?"

I kept expecting Ashton Kutcher to hop out at any moment. And then, Brooklyn kissed me.

I froze. I expected to snap back from reality and be standing in the baking aisle again, because this all was clearly a daydream. But no, this was real life.

Her game of chicken had ended with us crashing head-on. In the best way possible.

My heart pounded like a caged bird trying to escape, but I kept it under control as much as I could. She laughed and grabbed the bags and walked out of the store as I listened to Morrissey sing about that ten-ton truck being the most heavenly way to die.

Outside the store, she stared at me, waiting for me to say something. I didn't. I had no idea what I could say.

"What?" she asked. I took a deep breath and exhaled.

"We've been hanging out a lot on campus here lately."

"Caleb," she laughed.

"And I think you are great."

"Caleb," she continued.

"I just think I should tell you I'm not really in a space to commit to anything right now and I just wanted to be upfront with you and not waste your li-"

"Caleb!" She said, finally cutting me off.

"Yeah?"

"I'm looking at you because I don't know how to get to your grandmother's house and I am waiting for you to lead the way."

"Yeah, no, I was just worried, that, never mind." I bowed in the 'after you motion' in the direction we needed to walk, and my watch alarm went off again.

"Jeez, what did you have to remember so bad?"

"This stupid watch it goes off whenever it feels like."

"Well, what time is it?" she asked. I clicked the button on the side of the watch to illuminate the digital numbers.

"That's odd, it went off like twelve minutes ago and said two-thirteen."

She dug in her pocket and pulled out her phone and showed me the time. 2:13. We kept walking in an awkward silence until we reached the corner of the block.

"Hey, Caleb." Brooklyn broke the silence.

"Yeah?"

"How many women fall in love with you after kissing you?" She laughed as I chased her across the street and down the sidewalk.

When we got to my grandma's we were

immediately met with hugs and kisses, which
was a clear act put on by my grandmother.
My grandma is a very warm-hearted woman,
but her affection has to be earned. Once
earned, though, you are drowned in it.
There were new pill bottles on the little
wooden table near my grandmother's chair,
so I know she was getting ready to light
one up.

"Brooklyn, dear, do you partake?" my
grandma asked while shuffling slowly back
to her chair.

"Ma'am?"

"Grandma!" I said through my teeth. I
could feel the blood rushing to my cheeks
from embarrassment.

"Young man, do not talk over women,
it's very rude. Sorry, dear, sometimes I
think wolves raised him. I asked if you
smoked marijuana."

"Occasionally, yes, but I have a
better idea." She left me standing in the
foyer and walked over to where my grandma
was sitting. She sat on the arm of the
chair and held the pill bottle full of
joints up to her eye.

"I gave up cocaine in the seventies,
dear."

"Grandma!" I exclaimed. I could feel
myself melting through the floorboards from
shame.

"Don't worry, Mrs. Stevens—"

"Call me Granny, child," my grandma

interrupted with a smile.

"Okay, Granny," Brooklyn laughed.
"Caleb, can you see if you have any eggs?"
She threw me the bag full of brownie mix
and shook the bottle of joints.

"Wait a second, you wan—"

"Do you have a weed grinder, granny?"
Brooklyn interrupted me while leaning over
my grandma and sticking her tongue out at
me.

"No, she doesn't," I answered.

"Second drawer to your left under the
sink, Clark," my grandma replied.

"Wait, so your real name isn't Caleb?"

"Yes." I took a deep breath and slowly
exhaled all my embarrassment. "She calls me
that because Clark Kent's real name is
similar to mine."

"You mean Kal-El?" Brooklyn giggled.

"Yup, he's my Superman," my grandma
added.

"My hero," Brooklyn mocked me.

I got all the ingredients out that she
needed to bake, laughing at how ridiculous
this all was. When I turned from the
kitchen counter, I watched as Brooklyn
helped my grandma into the kitchen hand-in-
hand. I walked over and pulled out a chair
from the table for Grams to sit in. I sat
on the table beside her, and we watched in
amazement while Brooklyn worked her magic
to create weed brownies.

We listened to Brooklyn talk while she

was preparing. She told us that when her dad was stationed in Colorado, that's where she learned the recipe. She told us that baking was a sort of therapy for her, and she baked every chance she got. Her mom wasn't around when Brooklyn was younger, so she always did the baking for her dad. She told us that the best feeling in the world for her was when her dad would tell her that her cakes, pies and cookies tasted just like her mother's.

Even though the sentiment was sad, I envied her. The way she spoke about her parents was filled with so much emotion. I wanted that. To feel so connected to one thing that it just always brought me back to happy times with my parents. Would be even doper if that feeling was reciprocated.

Looking at my grandmother focusing on Brooklyn's words, I could tell she wanted that too. We lost track of time, lost in Brooklyn's words, and the brownies were finished in no time.

After the brownies were cooled, Brooklyn cut them into bite-sized pieces and warned us not to eat more than two. She gave me a separate warning to not eat more than a half of one, because they were for my grandma to take with her to chemo. Although I had recently fallen victim to peer pressure of cannabis, by my grandmother of all people, I just agreed

137

with Brooklyn's terms.

"Eat one on the way there and one while you're doing the procedure and you won't have an ounce of nausea," she told my grandma. I had never seen this side of Brooklyn before. Granted, we had only seen each other in school and a handful of times outside of that, but this I couldn't quite put my finger on.

"Brooklyn, baby, when are you coming back?"

"Whenever you will have me, Mrs.…"

"Granny, baby."

Brooklyn nodded and smiled at Gram's words. I followed her to the front door and started to feel déjà vu. Maybe it was from all the 90s movies where there's that awkward will-they-won't-they kiss. Or maybe it was just another glitch in the matrix.

Before I could say anything, Brooklyn stepped forward and hugged me so tight that I stood frozen, smelling her perfume that somehow lasted all day, feeling her heart beat in sync with my own. I even noticed the song "Poison" playing softly by Bell Biv DeVoe, but only because a car up the block was blasting it at a stop sign.

Foreshadowing? I wondered.

"Thank you," she whispered as she kissed me on the cheek. She walked off the porch and grabbed my bike.

"You're a thief now?" I joked.

"Come get it if you want it," she said

as she rode away.

"Well, she's a fast one yelling that out in public."

"She meant the bike, grandma."

"Oh." My grandma laughed as she left me at the door to go sit in her chair. I closed the door and walked in, expecting to see her lighting up. But instead she was reading a book. I started to walk upstairs when she stopped me.

"What are your intentions with this girl, Caleb?"

"I don't have any."

"Just remember, before you try fixing someone, make sure you aren't interrupting their karma."

"I'm not. I mean, I am just following your advice with enjoying the ride of life and all that. But she says things that just amaze me sometimes."

"All mazes do is lead to a bunch of dead ends if you aren't careful. That's all."

CHAPTER THIRTEEN

(83mi)

It's been a while since she and I had a moment like this. A moment when we had a chance to do nothing. We sat quietly in the park, listening to nature murmur to itself and the occasional car drive by.

We shouldn't have been here, considering everything that had happened, but I was selfishly enjoying this moment just as much—if not more than—her. Besides, I've never been the one to stop this woman from doing anything she wanted to do, and I'm not sure anyone could. I envied that about her.

The world could be on fire and she'd stand back and marvel at the flames like a fiery aurora borealis. Or she'd make shadow puppets on the wall from the light just to get a good laugh. The most accurate metaphors, I assure you. She can always find the silver lining in a cloud, even one made of smoke.

We sat in silence, but somehow I found her approval in it. I could feel her reading everything on my mind, or in my heart, and I know she was pleased with what she saw. I even envied that too, wishing I liked what I saw when I looked.

"What is it?" she asked.

"Nothing, just thinking."

"Well, don't hurt yourself," she poked.

"Ha ha," I replied in the most sarcastic voice I could.

"Admit it. I'm funny, even in my old age."

"Yeah, your old age is exactly why we should get you back inside. It's too chilly out here."

"Awh. Just a little while longer?" she teased through poorly exaggerated chattering teeth. I replied with a headshake of disapproval and a smile before I leaned over on her shoulder. The crisp morning air lingered around us as if it was waiting for the light of day to warm it. The sun peeked through purple and peach marble covers as it sleepily rose into the sky.

The creamy backdrop of dawn behind the hospital almost made it look like a peaceful place, making us forget how much we dreaded it. Since Grams's been spending more days in the week in the hospital than she has at home, she'll take any excuse she can to escape.

The park wasn't much, but it served its purpose, nestled between a Dairy Queen

and what seemed to be a graveyard of cars
in a forgotten parking lot of the hospital.
It sat across from the geriatric wing of
the building, so the kids getting dragged
with their parents to visit their
grandparents could play while their parents
and security watched them from the window.

Besides two benches, the park held a
jungle gym, a swing set, and a fountain.
Grandma liked to sit at her window and
watch kids almost kick each other from the
swings being a few inches too close. For
her it was like waiting for skateboarders
to wipe out.

I think I got my love of people
watching from her.

Looking over the massive windowpanes,
I saw a woman waving as if trying to get my
attention. I went to sit up and my grandma
clenched my hand.

"Don't look, Caleb."

"Huh, why?"

"She wants something, obviously. Just
ignore her."

Just then, two little girls, almost on
cue, raced out of the side entrance of the
building and over towards us. "See," she
continued, "Mom of the Year wants us to
watch her kids for her. No, let's go, we
are leaving."

"Grandma," I laughed. I waved and
pointed at the kids, letting her know I
would keep an eye out for them. "The

security guard starts his shift soon at
nine, and when he sees us, he's gonna drag
you back inside to get you ready for your
treatment."

"You sucker," she growled.

"Grandma, you like kids," I laughed.

"From a distance, yes, and now I can't
smoke the rest of this roach I've been
rationing all week because of these little
angels being out here."

Angels, I thought to myself. We
watched the kids thread themselves
throughout the colorful metal structure.
The parking lot slowly started to come to
life the higher the sun climbed into the
sky, and before I knew it, there were two
more kids out here. Grandma perked up as
her favorite game of swing versus kid
began. We watched the little girls push
each other on the swing while the little
boys stood on top of the jungle gym and
made faces at them.

"Innocent love."

"Love? Grandma, they are like six.
Don't wish such horrible things on them."

My grandma stood up and brushed
herself off. "Ohhh hush. You are never too
young or too old for heartbreak." But as
she spoke, she seemed distracted. I saw
her attention had zeroed in on something
across the parking lot. I looked over and
saw an interesting old man in hospital
scrubs with suspenders get out of a car. He

kissed the woman driving and waved at her
as she drove off, then walked to a patch of
flowers, picked three, and moseyed his way
through the hospital doors.

I thought I heard my grandmother
mumble 'son of gun' as she sat back down,
but I wasn't sure.

"You ready to go?" My question fell on
deaf ears. I waited a moment and watched
her face soften as I started to put two and
two together. "Grandma, who was that guy?"
I continued.

"Ohh, just a man."

I went to brush off my own question,
but she continued. "A man who thinks he's
cheating on his wife with me."

"Huh?" I blurted out with a rush of a
thousand questions.

"Yeah, her and I spoke about it once
when she decided to come to my room and
introduce herself. I had my suspicions, but
he had assured me she was dead and I
assured her I didn't mind."

"Grandma." I planted my face in my
hands with a slap.

"Turns out, she didn't mind, either.
We agreed to keep things as is. He makes us
both very happy, and we do the same for
him. That's all it's really about, being
happy."

"Wouldn't it be easier to just tell
him and be in a wholly poly—" I stopped. "I
can't believe I was just about to suggest

that."

"No, screw him, it's funnier this way to me and her. She's the one who brought over the potato salad last week."

"Guess you're right," I trailed off. I was so lost in the moment, I didn't notice when the security guard got near us. He held out his hand for my grandma to take as he helped her up. He began to lecture her about sneaking off, but she interrupted him.

"Do you mean that?" she asked me, stopping after taking a few steps.

"Yeah, I guess. If you are happy now and can look back and be happy later, carpe diem."

She pulled the security guard's arm down to bend him closer to her. She cupped her hand over his ear and whispered a very intentional loud whisper, "My grandson finally grew a pair, and learned what YOLO means."

I was gonna retort, but I just watched them laugh as they walked off. I sat on the bench in a bit of disbelief of myself. I'm sure I meant what I said, I just don't know why I said it. Maybe I'm just envious of getting to that point.

I watched the girls push each other back and forth on the swing and the boys taunt them from the jungle gym. I started to remember a time where Brooklyn and I would sit on these swings. Just as I was

smiling at the memory, one of the boys
slipped and the girl on the swing kicked
him off the jungle gym.

I stood up, jaw dropped, and ran over.
The kid sat up, rubbing his head.

"Are you alright?" I asked, looking
him over.

"Yeah. My arm hurts," he said, looking
behind me at the girl. I looked over at her
too, and she started crying at the top of
her lungs. I assumed her mother saw my
grandma leaving and came down to relieve me
of my impromptu babysitting shift, because
she raced over all distraught.

"What the hell did you do to my
daughter, you little pervert!" she
screamed.

"Hey, don't go calling kids perverts."

"I'm talking to you!"

"Me? Nobody did anything to your
little monster."

"Yeah! Monster," the kid mimicked me.

"Don't call girls monsters," I said,
helping him stand.

"He—he—" the girl said through tears,
pointing at the little boy.

"Apologize to my daughter," the mother
demanded.

"But I didn't do—"

I cut the kid off before he could
finish his plea. I kneeled down to him and
put my hand on his shoulder.

"Look, kid. For the rest of your life,

146

girls are gonna be doing things to hurt you, and you will have to apologize for it."

"But why?" he asked, choking back tears of confusion.

"Centuries of reinforcement." I looked up behind the kid and saw my grandma pointing and laughing. She pointed at the flower tucked behind her ear, blew me a kiss, and walked over to her bed.

"Sorry," the boy said as he stuck out his tongue at the little girl. I whipped my head around to look at the mom, but her back was turned, facing the little girl. Then, to no surprise, she stuck her tongue back at him and smiled. I looked at him, and he was smiling back.

The kid was doomed.

CHAPTER FOURTEEN
(**814mi**)

"I can not believe I let you guys talk me into this," I said in a fit of panic. I rocked back and forth, rolling the window down and gasping for fresh air. Realizing nobody answered me, I cried out again. "So now I'm invisible?"

"Dude, invisible means we can't see you, not that we can't hear you," Joelle said.

"Eh, I don't think that's entirely true," I responded.

"Yeah it is. What you're thinking about is mute," AJ chimed in.

"No, dude, that's when you can't talk, but we can still hear you," Joelle said confidently. We all paused, and then burst out laughing as he gave us looks of mock confusion.

"Your grandma is gonna be in the hospital all weekend, so it's the perfect time to go."

I hated when Joelle made sense, as he usually does. We were winding down this endless back road as if assassins were

148

chasing us. Joelle was a speed demon, but denied it every chance he got. When we got behind a tractor going five miles per hour, I took another drink from the bottle.

I sipped cautiously this time, closed my eyes, and focused on the burn as the liquid slid down my throat, relaxing my anxiety. Joelle lay on the horn until the guy moved over enough to get around, and then we were off again like a bat out of hell.

"Listen, Caleb, white guy to adjacent white guy, I have never been camping either, but I think we are pretty safe," AJ assured me.

"What do you mean 'think' and 'pretty safe?' Are there bears in these woods?" I fired back at him.

"There are absolutely bears in these woods," Joelle said, zipping around the tractor. "But he means if anybody dies, since I'm the black guy, I'll be the first to go."

"That's not what I meant, but a very good point made! See, Caleb, we are gonna be fine. It's just camping," AJ said, handing me a water bottle from the cooler he had up front. I took a huge gulp, then realized it was vodka. I coughed like a madman while he laughed hysterically.

I've had some of my favorite moments being with these two. They were the brothers I never had, and never knew I needed.

"Whatever. I guess it's not like the typical couples-go-into-the-woods type movie, and then everybody getting cabin fever."

"Yeeeaah, so about tha—"

"So, how long have you and Brooklyn been dating now?" AJ interrupted Joelle.

"Shut up, AJ. About what, Jojo?"

"So, you aren't denying the relationship," AJ persisted.

"There is no relationship. We are just friends who've hung out more and more recently."

"What is it about her that's stopping you?"

"Okay, well,

I don't like her laugh.

I don't like how she finishes my sentences, like I can't speak for myself.

I don't like how her perfume is always changing.

I don't like how she always manages to wear paint on her clothes.

I don't like her boring brown eyes.

And she doesn't wear a bra, and I think her tits are too symmetrical."

They paused and stared at me as if they didn't believe a word I said.

"Did he say too symmetrical?" AJ leaned over and whispered as if I wasn't sitting there.

"Yeah, too symmetrical. Like she was perfectly put toget— whatever."

150

"Yeah, okay, bud," AJ laughed. "You need to get you an older woman now. Those bodies are one to talk about."

"Dude, stop imposing your porn preferences on us," I joked. AJ rolled down the window and climbed halfway out to sit on the door.

"Dude, you're gonna mess up my door doing that one day," Joelle complained while pulling and hitting his legs. He turned down a dirt road and pulled into a small clearing where there were no trees. I reached up front and pulled the handle to the door AJ was sitting on, and it flung open, sending AJ to the ground. I think he was laughing harder than I was.

"Yeah, laugh it up until you guys wreck my baby," Joelle said, inspecting his passenger side door. I walked over to the hatchback and lifted it.

"Jesus, there is a lot of stuff in here," I said, fumbling through the bags.

"Can never be over prepared, I always say."

"AJ, I'm pretty sure you've never said that before just now, today," I mocked him.

"Yeah, but now it's what I'm gonna always say," he replied while dusting the dirt from his shorts. I started pulling stuff out of the back and tossing it to Joelle as he made a pile.

"Seriously, guys, this is a lot of stuff for one night. We should have invited

151

more people," I prompted.

"Yeah, yeah, simmer down," Joelle replied.

"He's wishing his girlfriend Brooklyn was here," AJ joined in.

"Yeah, if only."

"If only what, Caleb?" a voice said, freezing me in place with my head buried in the back of Joelle's car.

"Hey, babe," Joelle said to the approaching footsteps. I turned almost in slow motion and saw Hillary and Brooklyn with backpacks on walking down the cleared path.

"He was saying—"

"If only I had eaten before we came out here," I interrupted AJ.

"He's lying," AJ said with surgical precision, trying to light the campfire. "He was saying how he loved the movie *Cabin Fever* and is glad we are all here to act it out, or whatever." A flame shot up from the pile of firewood, almost burning his sideburns off.

After we finished laughing, the girls pulled out stuff to make s'mores. Brooklyn had weed brownies from the batch we had made a few days before. Soon, we were all high and enjoying the night. Talking about whatever came up for what felt like days—but was really just hours.

"That movie about five friends, two couples and a fifth wheel bozo, go into the woods to camp and the water is contaminated and they all get sick and die…" Brooklyn said out of the blue.

"Nice, Stevens," AJ said in a disappointed tone. "Good to know you think of me as a fifth wheel."

"Dude, she said that, not me," I laughed.

"All that talk about death Caleb was doing on the way here, and AJ's worried about being called a fifth wheel," Joelle said, picking up Hillary and spinning her in a circle.

"We have to keep our eyes on this one, guys," Brooklyn said, leaning over on me and falling out of her chair.

"Guys, y'all aren't looking at the bigger picture here. If Jojo and I are a couple and AJ is the fifth wheel bozo—" AJ picked up a pinecone and tossed it at Hillary, "—then he's considering him and Brooklyn as the second couplllleee," Hillary taunted. Everyone joined in with 'ooouus' and 'awwws' at Brooklyn and me.

"Alright, that's enough," I laughed. "I didn't even know you girls were coming, number one."

"Number two," Brooklyn interrupted, "he's afraid of love."

"I'm not afraid of it, I just don't believe in it. Being in love is like having your heart replaced with a cartoon bird that does whatever it wants for its own

153

amusement regardless of the outcome!" I exclaimed.

"We aren't talking about the tooth fairy or fairy tales here, Stevens."

"Thanks, AJ!" I barked at his betrayal. "How about I tell some scary stories about the New Jersey Devil?"

"AJ is enough devil we need here on this trip. So tell us, why are you so jaded?" Hillary asked, putting me on the spot. I couldn't help but think the brownies and these questions were planned long before this moment, but I was too baked to protest. I caved.

I started off light, easing them into my early woman woes. I told them about the bear that was taken from me when I was five by some random little girl. Even with me telling them this happened *on* Christmas, they didn't seem too moved by the story, even though I still had to choke back a tear. I moved on.

"It was Valentine's Day, and I was in the third grade now. I had spent all morning and all of recess working on this card to give to some girl (I pretended to not remember Maggie Churchill's name) at our Valentine's class party. It was in the shape of a cupcake and had cotton ball frosting at the top and a bunch of the letter U all over it, because on the back I had written "I'm sweet on u." Something, maybe now looking back at him, my pervy teacher shouldn't have told me to write, but I did. I couldn't wait until the actual party to deliver the card, so I had it passed down the row to her desk. She looked at it and smelled it and giggled at it with her friends. When the cupcakes arrived is when the party began, and we were able to roam around the room as we pleased. I went to walk over to her to tell her the card was from me, and that's when this blond devil ripped my heart out. When I got over to her, she was at Tony Staples desk (another name I pretend to forget), giving HIM MY card.

Not a card she had made in return for me. She gave him the card that I made. And what did he do? He ate it.

Fast forward to junior year of high school. Nikki Chung. We had started dating around the time a weird locker room rumor had been started amongst the girls in school after one of her basketball games. I would go to all her home games and cheer for her; she would come over to my house and beat all my friends AND me in video games. Then came prom. Nikki's friends were on the prom committee, so it was safe to say when they called her name for prom queen it wasn't a shock. The shock came when I went on stage to crown her, assuming I would get crowned next, but that didn't

happen. A senior, who was also on her
varsity team, was called to be the OTHER
prom queen. I stood five feet behind them
as they made out and slow danced on stage
in front of the entire school.

Then there was recently. I debated on
telling them, to avoid all the questions,
but I had already started putting the paint
on the canvas so I just decided to finish
the picture. I told them about the girl I
had been dating. Joelle's face lit up as I
was telling this story, as he remembered me
touching on this briefly before.

We met in a screenwriting workshop. It
started off friendly. I was instantly
attracted to her and asked her if she had a
boyfriend. She did. We were into almost all
the same things. We shopped at the same
stores, ate at the same places, and had
even been at the same concerts to see some
of our favorite acts, but had never met. We
had missed each other at every point we
should have met. We even both took the path
train in from Jersey to the city for this
class.

It felt like something in the ethos
had brought us together, me with my
reflection, even.

Because of the attraction, we only
hung out in class or got coffee at the ice
cream shop across the street. Whenever we
talked about her boyfriend, she always
sounded like she was trapped with him. She

told me she felt like she wasn't good enough to see a future with, but too good for him to break up with her and lose her. Whatever hold he had on her, I didn't pry on it. The walls kind of just came down naturally.

It seemed complicated, but we remained friends, ignoring the obvious attraction to each other. Then it turned from friends to me being an escape from her relationship. And then to random "luv ya's" when we would leave each other. No matter how much we tried to drown the phrase in a friendly tone, it didn't make it less complicating.

We had boundaries. We never texted, never had each other's numbers, social media, anything. Our situation was intoxicating. Eventually, we found ourselves never hanging out during our breaks in class or even after the class. We would, instead, find some dimly lit, abandoned stairwell in the building to have sex. Sometimes, if the yoga studio door was unlocked, we would use those mats, remembering to wipe them down after, of course.

The sex was passionate, amazing, and maybe even a little therapeutic. I assure you, us "dating" wasn't just in my head. Or maybe dating was the wrong word, but it was something.

We watched each other evolve as artists, even though we only saw each other twice a week. We helped change each other for the better and helped each other grow. Anyway, at some point one day I was walking to class, wondering to myself if she would leave him for me. I had bought some halal we could share during our break, because we never had time to leave and get food if we were busy doing other things.

When I got to class, I saw her showing the teacher and everyone there an engagement ring.

She looked at me swaying in the doorway. Time stopped for what felt like hours, but was in reality only a few seconds while we made eye contact.

Then she pretended to not see me and went back to accepting congratulatory praises and envious comments. The energy in the room shifted in a way, because there were people in the class that knew about us. I left and never went back to class after that, disregarding the opportunities I may have missed by not graduating.

I guess if I think about how much alike we were, I should have seen it could not work. Like, if we were truly that parallel, we were never meant to cross paths. In a plot twist kind of way, yeah, we changed each other. I changed her enough to be marriage material, and she changed me—"

"To be the Grinch of love and hate coffee? Holy shit, bro," AJ interrupted, jumping over the fire to hug me.

"Dude, you made the fire go out," I laughed. "And yeah, I guess that's why I hate coffee. I just drink tea. Kinda like an older song my Grandma was singing the other day by some English dude."

"You can be hurt for as long as you need to be. Nobody needs to rush you," AJ said.

"Shut up. I'm not hurt. And let me go."

"Yeah, Brooklyn, give it a rest," Joelle said, right before getting an elbow in the ribs from Hillary.

"Nice one, Hill," Brooklyn said, before walking off from the campsite.

"Babe, pillow talk stays where?" Hillary asked.

"On the pillows," she and Joelle said in unison.

"That's right," she continued. She got up to go after Brooklyn, but I volunteered to go instead.

CHAPTER FIFTEEN

I felt like I owed her an explanation, even if I simultaneously felt I didn't, because I didn't. I tried analyzing that 'give it a rest, pillow talk' exchange, but was still pretty ston-

"Caleb, what the hell!"

"Oh shit! Brooklyn, I'm sorry! I didn't mea-"

"What are you doing all the way over here!"

"I came to check on you because I thou—"

"Stop talking to me while I'm peeing!"

"Right." I walked away as quickly as I could and climbed a cluster of stones on a hill. I needed to see where we had made camp so I can get back there and pretend like this just never happened.

"Caleb," Brooklyn said, the murder and rage now gone from her tone.

"Yup."

"What are you looking for?"

"I was going to go back to camp and pretend I didn't see anyth—"

"You are looking in the wrong direction," Brooklyn laughed. She climbed on the rock and sat beside where I was standing. I balanced myself on her shoulder and sat down too.

"The Boy Wonder shouldn't use his hero powers for being a Peeping Tom," she said while throwing rocks in the water.

"Boy wonder?"

"Yeah. Clark is what your grandma calls you, right?"

"Robin is the boy wonder, Batman's sideki— Anyway, look. I just wanted to make sure you were okay from back there."

She kept tossing rocks into the water, ignoring the fact I was there. I wanted to say whenever people go off on their own in the woods in movies they get lost and end up having to eat one another to survive. I wish I hadn't mentioned the Jersey Devil earlier, because those stories felt way more real in this environment versus when you live in the city.

I also knew that if I mentioned any of this to Brooklyn, she probably would have thrown one of those rocks at my head.

"I'm not upset," she said softly.

"You aren't?" I asked, confused. Or maybe it was disappointment.

"No, I'm not. Usually when I make friends like you guys I end up leaving shortly after, so I guess I'm just anxious about that."

161

"Then don't leave, or do. You can find what you are looking for anywhere. You just have to give time, time."

"That's just it. Now that I have the option, I don't know what to do with myself. I never stayed anywhere long enough to get invited to the sleepover, or sync cycles with friends or date, and I thought you and I…" She trailed off.

The sun had started to set, and it had gotten considerably darker up on the rocks. I let her words surround me and give me what felt like an out of body experience. That's when I realized how amazing the scenery actually was, and how mesmerizingly beautiful she was, too. The trees were shedding their last few red and yellow leaves, and the ground was covered in a fiery blanket of leaf corpses.

"I just thought you were being nice by saying you hated love to spare the reality of not being into me," she continued. "I didn't know you were still fresh off of a breakup."

"Wasn't a breakup. We were never together."

"Caleb."

"Look, every love story is a tragedy if you wait long enough. It's just something that happens. I am into you. I just don't know how—"

"It's okay, Caleb," she said, leaning her head on my shoulder. We listened to the creek splash and plop around its banks as it ran off to join the dam. Cicadas hissed, birds chirped and beasts rustled in nearby bushes, waiting for the right moment to slaughter us, probably.

"I'm not just here to take care of my grandmother," I admitted. "My dad butt-dialed me a week or two before my grandmother called saying she was sick. He was in a therapy session."

"Therapy? Is he okay?"

"It was couples' therapy with my mom."

"Awh, that's great! They are working out their differences. See, not all relationships come to an abrupt stop."

"They've been divorced for almost two years now."

We sat quiet for a second until AJ howled in the distance, sending me flying off the rock.

"Easy, Clark." She pointed behind me at a fire.

"Excited bastard," I said, hunched over trying to catch my breath.

"Come on, Superman, let's head back," she said, holding me up by my arm.

"Before I could hang up the phone," I continued as we walked, "I heard the therapist say that you have to leave everything that's familiar to you, the stress, the normal, the good and the bad, to find a new you who can get a new perspective on the old. So I took her advice."

"Deep."

"So I'm here to find myself, and you're looking for a place to call home," I laughed.

"And then we found each other," she said, before letting go of my arm to run and tackle Hillary out of her chair.

"So Stevens, did you get any response from those applications?" AJ laughed as I joined everyone back at the campfire.

"Dude, what?"

"The jooooobs. Did you get any emails about the jobs? Did you get any jobs?" he continued.

"My phone's been right here with you guys the whole—" I stopped talking once he started to make a hand motion for a blowjob. The girls didn't see.

"Still unemployed," Joelle chimed in, answering for me.

"What about…" AJ motioned for hand job, but Brooklyn saw him this time and charged him, chasing him around the campfire.

"Kids, please. We just got this fire up and burning. Relax!" Joelle exclaimed. We all sat around the fire drinking Red Apple Ale AJ had stolen from his job at the gas station. Surprisingly enough, he had also stolen an entire box of hot dogs for us to cook around the fire.

"Jojo, this is why he wouldn't come in the store with us to buy buns and cups," I said, laughing.

"All these stores in town and you jerks wanted to go there," AJ complained.

I saw Hillary wrap her arms around herself and move closer to the fire, so I got up from my chair and grabbed a blanket from my bag. I handed to her.

"Dude?" Joelle said. "Get your own girl."

"Shut up, babe," Hillary came to my rescue. "This gesture was more for Brooklyn than it was me," she said, scooting her chair closer to Brooklyn's to share the blanket.

"No, it's not that," I laughed. Joelle stood up and wrapped his arms around AJ, then snapped his fingers at the girls.

"Fine, I upgraded anyway, booboo," he said in the most feminine voice he could.

Then Hillary took Brooklyn by the chin and gave her a peck on the lips.

"Is this about to be a classic scene of *American Pie 2?*" the nerd in me blurted out.

"Winner chooses the tents," Brooklyn proposed.

"Deal!" AJ shouted, as Joelle took off his glasses. AJ turned his hat backwards and did a few jumping jacks. They looked at each other and grimaced.

"Uh oh, ladies and gentlemen, battle of the sexes," I commentated. They slowly leaned into each other. "Guys, please, come on now, nobody wants—"

And before I could finish my sentence, Joelle leaned in really fast and kissed AJ. They both coughed and spit and shook in disbelief. The girls and I could not stop laughing. Then Brooklyn threw off the blanket. Her hand moved slowly until she grabbed Hillary by the chin and looked at me. Hillary put her hand on Brooklyn's boob and looked at Joelle.

"No fucking way," he whispered. The girls giggled, and then slowly leaned in and made out. Nobody said a word as we watched in amazement. It was the hottest thing I'm sure any of us had seen in person.

"Okay, that's it. That's enough," Joelle broke the silence. He walked over and pulled Hillary away from her seat and started kissing her, sending her into a fit of laughter.

I sat down in Hillary's chair and looked at Brooklyn while she cried winner because of the interference.

"Awh, come on dude, we could have won that," AJ complained.

"Are you kidding me? I am not making out with you, bro," Joelle replied.

"Looked a little jealous there for a second, Superman," Brooklyn whispered in my ear while AJ and Joelle went back and forth about whose fault it was that they had lost.

"Maybe I was," I replied, looking into her eyes. I suddenly realized that we were about to kiss.

But right before we could, we were interrupted.

"Hey, I have to go pee," Hillary said to Brooklyn.

"I'll be back," Brooklyn said, giving me a quick peck on the cheek.

"Babe, where's the TP?" Hillary yelled over Joelle and AJ's argument.

"I think it's in the back seat," Joelle replied, tossing her the keys. They sat down back around the fire and stared at me.

"What?" I asked

"What do you mean, what?" Joelle said.

"Dude, you guys clearly like each other," AJ continued.

"Yeah?" I asked

"What, are you high, dude? Date that girl. She's into you, bro," Joelle demanded.

"Maybe he has another girl in Jersey, Jojo,"

"No, I don't have another girl. I don't know what we are, but it's nice. If it becomes more than just friends, I think I'm open…" I stopped talking as the girls returned, laughing, and stood in front of us.

"I wanna hear the joke," Joelle prompted.

"You won't like it when you hear it," Hillary replied. We all looked at each other, unprepared for whatever they were going to say next.

"We lost the keys near the creek where we went to pee. So you boys have to share a tent and us girls will share the other," Brooklyn said. We laughed, until we realized they weren't joking.

"I wasn't going to sleep out here in the open woods. I was gonna sleep in the car. That's why there are only three tents!" I yelled.

"I call a tent to myself. Jojo should have to sleep with Caleb on the count of it's his fault we lost," AJ added.

"Sorry, boys. The third tent is locked in the car," Hillary said while grabbing her sleeping bag.

"Babe, you serious?" Joelle asked, very concerned.

"Night boys. Don't let the bugs bite, Caleb," Brooklyn mocked while grabbing her sleeping bag and followed Hillary into the tent. Joelle, AJ and I all looked at each other in shock while a gust of wind blew out the flame on the campfire.

Later, we all lay wide-awake in the tent, hating our lives while hearing the girls laughing across from us.

"You think they are doing all that giggling because—"

"Dude. Don't," Joelle demanded,

cutting AJ off. Leaves rustled around the tent from the wind and a classic owl hoot echoed throughout the woods.

"Go camping, they said. It will be fun, they said," I mumbled.

"You will sleep outside for that negativity, mister," AJ replied.

CHAPTER SIXTEEN

That next morning, Joelle woke up AJ
and me to help look for the keys. I looked
at my watch and read 8:45 a.m. I could tell
he'd been up for a while. I grabbed a new
shirt out of my bag and stuffed my feet
into my Vans, then crawled from the tent.

"AJ, dude, come on. Dad's waiting," I
laughed. AJ came out of the tent, laughing
and flipping his shirt inside out.

"Dad's waiting," he repeated, laughing
even harder than before. We reached the
area near the creek where he was standing.

"Caleb, you search near that tree. AJ,
you—dude, did you not bring any extra
clothes?" AJ looked down at the backwards
outline of the Biggie Smalls iron-on on his
now inside-out shirt.

"It's all good, baby, baybay," AJ
taunted in the worst Biggie Smalls
impression I ever heard.

"Dude, never ever say that again," I
told him. The girls walked up looking like
they had just left the spa. They even
smelled good.

"Um, did you guys take a shower or

something this morning?" AJ read my mind.

"What are y'all doing? Out here?" Hillary asked.

"Seriously?" Joelle asked, annoyed. "The keys, Hill."

"Oh no, That was just a joke. We had them the entire time," Brooklyn said. Hillary pulled the keys out of her bra and twirled them around her finger.

"We are leaving," Joelle said, storming off.

"Honey, come on, it was a joke," Hillary said, chasing behind him laughing.

"Really, bro? You thought that was funny?" AJ lectured me, because I couldn't stop laughing. "Someone's feet stank all night."

"Dude, that was your feet!" I cried. "Besides, be mad at Brooklyn and Hillary at their evil genius sexes scheme."

We all sat by the fire and roasted Pop-Tarts.

"So, what's everybody's plans after school?" Hillary asked the group.

"This isn't high school, babe. This is after school."

"Yeah, JoJo, but this isn't the end," AJ chimed in with an out-of-the norm serious tone. "This whole criminal justice thing my dad wants me to do isn't for me. I'm going to be a coach for high school, and then at a college level. I wanna be better than Coach K, have an extra letter

171

than him and everything."

Everyone kind of looked at AJ, waiting for him to say something, well, AJ-like right then. But he didn't. He just continued on his miniature wood cabin made of sticks. He would stack one and reach from around him and stack another, placing rocks wherever they needed to be.

Brooklyn stood up and gave a sarcastic applause. "Who knew he actually had a brain in that kneecap-shaped head."

"Ha ha," AJ said, holding up a middle finger while placing another stick on the wall of the cabin.

"Anyway, I want to be a famous painter," Brooklyn continued.

"That's it?" Joelle laughed, receiving an elbow to the ribs from Hillary.

"No, it's fine, Hill. Yeah, that's it. I think I've gotten so used to not being in one place for so long that I don't want to limit myself any one place. I've gotten some really good inspiration from being here, and want to harness as much of it as I can to eventually take with me. I just have to give time, time." She finished with a glance in my direction.

"That's beautiful, Brooklyn," Hillary said before she continued. "I'm going to open up my own bake shop. Maybe even incorporate some of the weed-infused things I've learned from you, Brooklyn. Besides me baking with my grandma since I was little,

172

I've been doing culinary classes while getting a master's in business. I just need to figure shit out from there."

"You guys are great and all," Joelle said, kissing Hillary on the cheek, "but I don't know or care at this point." Joelle laughed and walked over to inspect AJ's house project.

"Girl, you are okay with that?" Brooklyn asked.

"Hell yeah, she better be. Because wherever she goes, I'm going. I've gotten seven certificates this semester—refrigeration, electric, plumbing and stuff. And my dad owns a construction business. I can kinda do whatever I want, wherever she wants me to."

"That sounded like a plan to me, bro," AJ said, taking the stick Joelle was handing him. "Brooklyn, why do you sound so shocked? I would expect that from Stevens before you."

"Well, what about you, Caleb?" Brooklyn asked.

"I mean whatever makes them happy, I guess. I think they are great toge—"

"No," she interrupted. "Your plans. Besides Hollywood."

It took me a minute to find the words after Brooklyn's Hollywood comment. I felt apprehensive sharing my dreams, because they were already being poked at. "I applied to this program overseas that can land me an opportunity to pitch my script on a YouTube series. They have funding, just no ideas, but they know they want it to be a romantic dramedy."

"That's great!" Hillary screamed. She ran over and hugged me. "I'm a great actress, Caleb, if you are looking for a quirky best friend for the female lead."

"Sorry, Caleb. She's been watching too much *Broad City*," Joelle explained.

"YAS QUEEN," both Brooklyn and Hillary said at the same time.

"Yeah, well it's a slim chance, but it's possible."

"Is that recommendation you were telling me about for this?" Brooklyn recalled.

"Yeah."

"Well, why the hell wouldn't you get it?" Hillary asked.

"I told you guys yesterday, I haven't been back to that screenwriting class or reached out to even see if I qualified for their certificate, since I left early."

"Too painful."

"Shut up, JoJo," I laughed.

"Nah man, I get it. We will help you figure it out, though," he assured me as he put his hand on my shoulder and led us on an impromptu hike.

We started walking up the stream, trading stories from jobs we'd had in the past. The sun was finally starting to come out, extinguishing the morning crisp in the air. This is nice, I thought.

Brooklyn and I walked a few steps behind the rest of the group, both anticipating what the other was going to say.

"I would love to see that series once you produce it," she said, while wedging her hand in between my arm and white t-shirt.

"Well, I have to write it first. Maybe a bodega owner has a crush on a customer, I don't know," I laughed.

"Probably would just have a bunch of bodega sandwiches lying around, huh?" She joined me in laughing.

"Hanging out with you is like watching my favorite show," I told her.

"Oh yeah? What episode are we on?" she asked.

"I would saaaay… Season one, episode eight. The episode right before we have sex."

"Oh, really now?" she said, pushing me in the shoulder.

"Hell yeah. I meeean, I haven't seen the new episode yet, so I'm not really sure what will happen," I replied rather smoothly, if I do say so myself.

"Well, you need a healthy example of a relationship so you can write the series from both perspectives," she suggested.

"Okay, what movie you have in mind?"

"I meant us. We could just date for pretend. I can take direction, Mister Director."

"I don't know, Brooklyn."

"Me either, but that's the point. Just give time, time, Clark Kent. I'll be your Mary Jane."

"Lois Lane is Clark Ken— Never mind. Okay, fine, let's do it," I agreed.

Just then, Brooklyn stopped in front of me, took my cheeks in both her hands and kissed me. When she let my face go, I was floating over the treetops.

"Hey, guys!" Brooklyn called out ahead of us, snapping me back to reality. "When is the first day of winter?" she asked the group.

"September twenty-second, I think," Hillary replied.

"Winter is coming, winter is coming." AJ galloped through the two of us doing a horrible *Game of Thrones* impression.

"Hmmm, looks you are two weeks off, Clark. This is season two, episode one of our resear'lationship," Brooklyn said.

"That's a mouthful."

"Is it?" she asked, making me weak in the knees. I finally knew what SWV meant when she was singing it.

We all walked until we got to the top of this huge ledge of a reservoir and stared out at what looked like an oil painting. Brooklyn and I were the only ones

176

in awe. Probably because we didn't grow up around stuff like this all our lives, so it was refreshing.

"Hey guys! Bob Ross! Get it?" Hillary said to Brooklyn and me.

"Huh?" I replied.

"You two are always going on about 90s stuff, so I watched this painter dude on Netflix, and this is like a Bob Ross thing."

"Awh, girl, you did research to try and bond closer to me. I love you," Brooklyn said, running over to hug Hillary.

"You girls are so dramatic," Joelle said. Hillary elbowed him. Brooklyn took a ton of pictures of every angle she could get. I just imagined Bob making all types of sound effects while he stroked the brush over the canvas to make the wispy clouds in the sky. And then dabbing the bottom in random places with his brush in different reds and oranges and hints of greens.

"I used to hate when he would do something with the painting and you would be like 'damn it, Bob you ruined it' and then it would be perfect at the end," Brooklyn said, almost reading my mind.

"Yeah, like with the trees he'd do a bunch of random brown-grey lines and you'd be like 'what?'" I replied.

"Yeah, and then he would take his brush and just tap it over the canvas and you have that 'Aha!' moment," Brooklyn finished my thought.

"I'm annoyed I understand the language you guys are speaking, but you're sooo cute together," Hillary said.

"Guys, can we just snap some pics of me in this tree?" AJ asked while posing with one arm in the air.

"You wanna be a monkey so bad," Joelle mocked him.

"Whoa, that's offensive," AJ replied. Brooklyn circled us, talking and joking and taking pictures. Then Joelle took the camera and took some with Brooklyn in the candid shots. Finally, AJ climbed up in a tree and set the camera up for a group photo. After about seventy seconds of us posing, there was no flash or indication a photo was taken.

"Are you sure you set the timer?" Brooklyn asked him.

"I'm positive," he said. He went to grab the camera, and it started firing off shots. We all ran back in position, changing up poses and laughing. I've never had that much fun being earthy in my life.

As we walked back to our tents, our stomachs growled like savages. All I could think was, I could definitely get used to doing things like this. We all finally got back to the campsite and started cleaning, then turned on our phones and started checking every social media we had.

Everyone except me. I called my

grandma, and she hadn't even noticed I was missing. But she did instruct me to bring her home some food.

Hillary decided to drive and let Brooklyn sit up front while the guys piled in the back. AJ wanted to stop at his job to get food, but we were all hot dogged out. We agreed to get food from the deli in the grocery store uptown. Brooklyn had to clock in for work soon anyway, so it was a win-win.

When we pulled into the lot, Brooklyn jumped out and ran into the store before us. I walked around the store to try and find her after I got my chicken, to say bye or something. I didn't know what we were, but I knew 'friends' wasn't quite the right label for it. Just when I was about to give up my search, I got to the dairy aisle and she came from behind one of the freezer doors with her lunchbox.

"Just got to work and gonna take a lunch?"

"Bite me, Superboy," she laughed. When we got up front, she rang me up at the service desk. I turned to say bye to AJ before he left the store, and turned back around to a mischievous look on Brooklyn's face.

"What?" I asked, laughing.

"Nothing. Byeeeee," she said while walking around from the service desk to get on register. I grabbed my bags, but before

I could get out the doors she called out to me.

"Hey, Clark?"

"Yeah?" I answered. She didn't look up from scanning items.

"Never mind," she said, giggling while giving the lady she had just rung up her change. I threw my hand back, waving as I walked through the automatic doors. Halfway home, I realized I had an extra bag amongst my food. Before I turned around to bring the bag back to the store, I opened it and saw it was a small can of iced coffee. I then noticed on my receipt a message written in pink pen.

"I hate coffee now, too, so here, it's for grandma. BK Girl." She had drawn a little heart before her name at the end.

That must have been why she went and got her lunchbox out of the back room. I couldn't help but smile reading that note. I pulled out my phone and saw a missed call from my grandma. I called her back while I continued to walk, anticipating the fussing she was going to do for not answering her call.

"Hey gra- Well, yeah, I'm almo- Grandma, I didn't forget I have the food. I'm almost hom- Grandma!" I shouted, looking like a crazy person on the sidewalk. "I got you iced coffee. Okay, love you, too."

'Thanks, Brooklyn', I thought.

CHAPTER SEVENTEEN
(76mi)

I feel like I just made a deal with the Devil. Am I really desperate? Well, apparently I am. Do I see a long term or future with it? Not really. Do deals with the Devil ever end maybe not so bad? Not sure.

Regardless of the repercussions later, I needed a job. I mean, I already had a job I had been slacking on for weeks, but maybe upping my workload is the madness I need to get me on the right track.

Though, has madness ever gotten anyone on the right track?

Walking quickly trying to work off my nerves, I opened my phone to see if there was an undo button on the website. Suddenly, I bumped into something flannel-clad and sweaty stepping out of a store.

"Mr. Stevens!" Dr. Baldwin bellowed, juggling the food in his arms.

"Mr. Baldwin. Sorry about that. I was just—"

"Always with your head besides where it should be," he laughed.

"Hot date?" I jabbed back, touching one of the many bags he was carrying.

"Why, actually," he said, clearing his throat and caught off guard by my question. "Yes. I'm surprising my wife with a movie night. I got some food, already know what movie, now just need to head to the drug store."

"Oh, that's nice. Well, I hope she feels better," I said, while inching away to end the conversation.

"Oh no, she's not sick. I just picked up a little something to make the night better," he said, shaking the little pharmacy bag. I stood and looked at him purposely in an awkward blank stare of silence.

"Shared a little bit too much there, didn't I?" he said.

"Yeah. Just a tad," I answered. He nodded awkwardly and walked away. Considering his whole situation with his wife, his plans and overall joy consumed me. His wife loves/loved someone else. He loves her. I guess it's cool they are working/worked it out, but why? What about the other woman and her feelings, or does it serve her right to be left…

I shook my head and laughed. I wanted to say 'told ya so,' but to who? Nobody was listening. At some point even I stop listening to myself.

I turned, and realized that Mr.

Baldwin had been exiting one of my favorite sandwich shops. It was the second-best thing to a sandwich from a bodega, and I used to come here all the time. The names of the dishes were just as entertaining as the combinations of food that went in them.

I contemplated going in, but I couldn't bring myself to do it. For weeks, I even avoided walking down this side of the street, just because of this place.

I turned to continue down the street, feeling defeated, when life decided to do that funny thing it always does to me. The owner opened the door and walked out and hugged me.

"Caleeeeebb," he stretched in his super-thick, Long Island accent. "You were gonna come by my shop and not say hello? What's the matter with you?"

"Tony," I grunted, getting crushed in between his hairy bicep and greasy apron. "No, I just didn't have my debit card, so I didn't wanna even-"

"Come on, for you? Lunch is on Tony," he said, referring to himself in the third person. I followed him into the shop and down memory lane. Nothing had changed, except the white bar stools at the counter now had navy pinstripes to go with his mural of the Yankees that hung on the wall. The same ESPN radio station was playing, the same photoshopped pictures of Tony with celebrities hung on the walls, and the

183

heavenly smell stank up the air. It was great.

"You take a seat. I'll be right with you," Tony instructed. I sat down, and right before my brain went into a dream sequence of the times I used to be here, finally something stuck out that was different. I looked up and read today's specials, confused.

"Yo, Tony," I said in an unintentional New York accent.

"Sorry, boss. How can I help you?"

I pointed at the special menu, and he hung his head in shame. "What happened to the theme of the Today's Specials?" I asked.

"I know, I know. It's a long story."

"I got time," I said, resting both arms on the counter.

He exhaled and set down the rag he was holding, then walked over from behind the counter to sit beside me on a stool.

"To make a long story a little less long," he said, lowering his voice. "Some detective comes in here asking me about one of my customers, shows me a picture of the guy. A creepy guy, I admit, but loyal. Said I recognized him, next thing I know, cops are staking out the joint waiting for the creep guy, not even ordering the food, just a bunch of coffee, until finally the creep comes in. They bust him and tell me he was buying things off my menu, like three or four of the same thing at once, and then taking it to women's homes and jobs because they reminded him of them, like some weird Buffalo Bill or Leatherface stuff. Some sick shit."

"Really sick shit," I agreed.

"And that detective bastard, excuse my language, tried to say I was in on it. Called me a weirdo because he didn't understand my humor. He's lucky he had a badge, or I'd put him in one of these pots back there."

"That's crazy," I said, not knowing what else to say.

"Yeah it is. So now it's just numbers on the menu until I figure out something else to do," he said with a sad tone. "But I can make you anything you want. You tell me and I'll cook it up." He jumped up and got behind the counter and put on his plastic gloves.

"Well, I have been craving a chop cheese."

"Is that like a grilled cheese?" he asked. I was completely questioning his New York card after that, though granted he was an older Long Islander.

"No it's like a Philly cheesesteak, but better."

"Sorry, pal. I hate Philadelphia, and everything and anything that has to do with Philly. How about I surprise ya."

"Cool," I shrugged. He started on a

rant about how Rocky, yes, the made-up
boxer, was actually born in Long Island and
that's where his hate stems from. He
reminded me of Grams in the way he could
cycle through thoughts like wildfire. He
went from Rocky to how he actually knew
Forrest Gump, and then how his dad owned
the diner that Seinfeld ate at on the show.

Also like Grams, it was hard to tell
what pieces were true in his stories, but
they were usually entertaining, so it
didn't matter.

Before I knew it, he was done with my
dish: grilled shrimp with cherry tomatoes,
cucumbers, and chives that he let steam
under a cooking pot top on the grill. He
added that to a Hawaiian bread hero and
sprinkled it all spices, a pinch of seaweed
flakes, and crushed sunflower seeds. Then
he gave me a saucer of Thousand Island
dressing. My mouth watered uncontrollably
as I picked up this masterpiece.

"What do you think I should call this
one?" he asked, right after I took a bite.
My mouth was full, clearly, so he continued
to talk. "I was thinking maybe the Mermaid,
if I was gonna add it to the menu. I was
also thinking maybe the Hawaiian."

"Yeah. Maybe a places theme could be
your new angle," I said, finally able to
reply.

"Speaking of, where's that pretty face
you used to come in here with all the

time?" he asked. I was glad I had swallowed whatever food I had in my mouth to avoid choking on the subject at hand.

"What girl?" I stalled.

"What girl… Your grandmother, that girl," he mocked back. "I thought when I stopped seeing you lovebirds that maybe you had flown off and married or something."

"No. No marriage. No flown off anywhere. No nothing," I said, steadily stuffing food in my mouth hoping it would buy me time to think.

"Awh, pal." He placed his hand on my shoulder, leaving all types of greasy residue and crumbs.

"No, it's fine."

"Of course it's fine! Her loss."

"Who said she broke up with me?" I defended.

"Hey, no judging, kid. I get it. The way you used to be mesmerized by her looks. Everything is going fine and then bam—life happens. Say no more."

I couldn't have agreed more. That's what happens to most relationships, life. Sometimes life is just the two separate ones fusing together and making one super-life. Other times it's a cancer, and you realize, 'Hey maybe we should jump ship before this kills both of us.' Some people make it back from the dead, like the dean and his wife.

"Hey, kid!" Tony called out while I

was eating the last bite of the sub. He printed a receipt, ripped it out of the machine and tore it into pieces. "This one's on me."

"Yeah, thanks," I said sarcastically, forgetting the free food was the whole reason I was there anyway. I got up and dug in my pocket for the few dollar bills I had and left them on the counter.

For the first time leaving Tony's, I felt worse now than I did before coming in. Usually I'm smiling ear-to-ear with a food baby I'd be carrying around for the rest of the day. Now, I'm only carrying the thought that I don't really know what happened with Brooklyn and me.

I thought everything truly was fine. Maybe that's the ten-ton truck Morrissey was singing about when he was saying there was a light that never goes out.

Maybe that truck was "life" for that couple too.

CHAPTER EIGHTEEN
(588mi)

I sat at the sandwich shop, waiting for my friends to show up. Of course I knew they would be late, which is why I got here thirty minutes after the time we agreed. Which meant they should be here in only another ten minutes or so.

AJ hit the group chat and said in order to prove I was still their friend, I had to order exactly what they would eat off the specials menu. A challenge I was determined to pass.

I looked up at the specials and smiled at the theme. I laughed, thinking to myself which girl was right for them as I read the tag line to the menu.

Sit down with one of these girls for a taste of a lifetime.

THE MARIA: ROTISSERIE CHICKEN, ROAST PORK, PICKLES, PEPPER JACK CHEESE, SWEET PEPPERS AND SPICY MUSTARD
THE CHARLIZE: FOUR CHEESE MAC AND CHEESE GRILLED CHEESE WITH BLUE CHEESE

ON A PANINI
THE ANGIE: PISTACHIO BUTTER, NUTELLA,
& JELLY ON TWO BLUEBERRY WAFFLES
Soup of the day
THE SAMANTHA: TOMATO, BASIL, SHRIMP
AND CRUSHED PRETZEL SOUP

I wouldn't dare sit down with any of these mouth grenades myself, but I ordered for them anyway. I pulled out my computer to finish up some lines on a new scene I was writing. I hadn't been writing much lately, so any chance I got to myself, I tried to. But I was distracted.

I watched two dogs through the window beside me. One was a fluffy white dog with a pink, studded collar chained to a mailbox, which I assumed was waiting for her owner. The other dog was a brown dog with a blue scarf that was doing everything it could to get Trixie's attention. I didn't know if that was the dog's name, but that's what I named her for now. Standing on his back legs, rolling over, and even playing dead, nothing made Trixie's eyes move from the glass doors to the restaurant.

Right when Samson was going to walk away (yes, that's the name I gave the other dog), it's like a light bulb went off in his head.

"Stevens!" AJ shouted, as if he had been trying to get my attention for a while.

"JoJo! AJ!" I screamed like a little schoolgirl. We grouped-hugged like long-lost brothers before we sat down. Conveniently, Samantha and Maria showed up at the same time. Joelle pulled the soup in and AJ did the same with the Maria before passing me half.

"Told you he'd get you the one you wanted," Joelle said.

"Lucky guess. Hey, look who's writing again!"

"Yeah. I've been writing this paragraph for what seems like weeks, but I'll finish it later."

"Why aren't you finishing it now, bro? We can wait." Joelle encouraged. It was a nice change of pace, I realized. I had been spending a lot of time with Brooklyn, and she too often seduced me into doing my writing later.

"Nah, you guys deserve all my attention. I feel like it's been forever."

"I know. Did you witness that hug just now?" Joelle said, slurping tomato all over his white Odd Future shirt. "That was a hug of people who haven't seen each other in forever."

I half-listened to him as I looked out the window and noticed Samson had almost chewed through Trixie's leash. He now had her attention.

"JoJo, he's not listening," AJ said, bringing me back into the conversation.

191

"Guys, sorry. I've just been working, I guess you can say."

"Working or boo'd up?"

"They are one and the same," I told them, taking a bite of my half of Maria. I thought about how in the short time I've known AJ, he's always split his sandwiches with me. Never asked if I wanted some, or if I was hungry. He just gave me half. Partly because he said I needed to beef up more. Partly because Joelle never finished his food, but was too stubborn to order anything less than everybody else, or maybe because he saw me as a little brother. We were brothers.

"Didn't think you would be one of the guys who gets a girlfriend and ditches his friends," Joelle said, waving the waiter over.

"We haven't hung out really since we went camping, and that was almost two months ago."

"Wrong, AJ," I corrected. "JoJo and I saw each other last week at the grocery store while Hillary and Brooklyn picked up some things."

"Dude, you've been seeing Caleb behind my back?" AJ nagged Joelle.

"It was just the once. It meant nothing," he laughed.

"Honestly, guys, I'm sorry. I know we were trying to hang out a few times here and there and see some movies I wanted to review, but Brooklyn has had me busy."

"Does sound like more work than a relationship," AJ replied. He pulled Joelle's half-eaten soup from in front of him and unwrapped his spoon.

"Dude. I have a cold," Joelle said.

"Yeah, one I gave to you. I just got over that."

"Okay, well, I have mono then."

"Yeah, I gave that to Hillary, so—" Joelle punched him in the shoulder before AJ could finish insinuating.

We laughed and caught up on each other and what's been going on. Which I didn't know how needed it was until it was happening. I felt out of the loop, which I hated even though they didn't share too much on themselves. It was enough to make me envious, for sure. All they wanted to know was more about Brooklyn and me. Joelle brought up how Hillary told him about me helping Brooklyn during her baking competition. Which brought up an entire slew of Caleb Crocker jokes and questions about what color apron I had on. I shamelessly left out happily playing house. That day was great, throwing flour around, splashing each other with batter, smearing frosting on each other, my horrible Gordon Ramsey impersonation.

That day spilled into a fun few days, since everything we baked was edibles.

Her Facetiming her dad so I could meet

him while he was away.

Us making a joint email address so we could share a Netflix and Spotify account.

Finding the perfect synergy of her paintings and my photos.

It definitely was interesting, for the lack of a better word, having Brooklyn as a tutor. She actually showed me how to hotwire a car, because her dad showed it to her when she was six. I still cross a few wires here and there, but our Bonnie and Clyde roleplay was definitely fun.

Then it was the carnival. I talked Brooklyn into riding the Ferris wheel, even though she was afraid of heights. It was great. Us sitting at the top, people watching over the whole park, taking some pretty dope pictures. The pictures were for her to paint the different scenes later— that idea help smooth over the fact we were up there longer than anticipated. We ate junk food until our stomachs hurt, and left with a giant stuffed animal. I even completely forgot about our movie I had bought tickets for because we were having such a good time.

I told them Brooklyn had invited me to meet some of her friends at a few parties coming up, and that she was planning a road trip of some sort for us. For me, this little event meant so much more than what it was on the surface. This a girl who whenever asked about anything personal would give the most generic answer possible. Not to be purposefully mysterious, or difficult, but because she felt like she genuinely didn't know herself, therefore had nothing to share. If she had actually made friends in other places where she honestly remembers nothing of her life there besides her address, of course I would be ecstatic to meet them.

The guys looked at me in shock.

"So you are like full-on in this thing," Joelle reaffirmed.

"Yeah," I answered, unsure of myself. "I mean, it's just you know, experience for my writing."

"But you haven't been doing much posting for your movie reviews to your channel, and even flaked on us a few times when we said we would go with you," AJ said.

"It's been a little crazy getting into the groove of everything, that's all. Maybe she's the girl that's gonna come along and grant all my wishes."

"Manic Pixie."

"The hell is Manic Pixie?" AJ asked.

"A Manic Pixie dream girl is a cute chick whose main purpose is to sorta inspire a greater appreciation for life in the main character. In our case, Caleb," Joelle replied.

"Dude. Brooklyn is not a Pixie Dream girl," I defended, the very little part of

195

his explanation I thought he was wrong about—because everything else was spot on.

"She's definitely Manic," AJ said.

"Do you even know what Manic means?" I asked him.

"No. Like crazy, I guess. She lives in her own world and does whatever she wants. What on that list of things you guys have been up to was something you chose to do?" AJ replied. I paused, taking a second to digest everything that had been said up until now.

"It's not about that. You're the one who told me to date the girl. I've been against relationships forever!"

"He's right, AJ. But to my point, Caleb's in his own world too, like a movie. You and Brooklyn are both joyriding in each other's journeys," Joelle concluded.

"Joyriding sounds like a good time."

"Until you run out of gas," AJ snarked while calling the waitress over.

"Or until he runs into a dead end," Joelle added, flicking a shrimp tail over at me. AJ was just going to order a side of fries when we saw the waitress drop her note pad. She stared with a mixture of shock and anger out the window.

We looked to see what was so shocking. First thing I noticed was the chewed leash swinging from the mailbox. Then, AJ pointed out the two dogs stopping traffic, rolling around, playing in the street.

"They are gonna get each other
killed," Joelle said uncharacteristically.

"No, man. Samson freed her. This chick
was at work, so no telling how long Trixie
was out there. He's a hero."

"Stevens, why do you know the dog's
name?"

"More importantly, stop projecting,
bro, they're dogs. He's no more of a hero
than Icarus if they keep flying that close
to the sun," Joelle finished. I loved his
metaphor too much to offer a rebuttal.

Then I couldn't stop wondering if I
was in fact projecting.

CHAPTER NINETEEN

(**51mi**)

"Dude, you are doing that stare-off-into-space thing."

"JoJo? What are you doing up here?"

"Well, we came to visit your grandma, and the nurse said you were around but she didn't know where. Then your grandma said you would probably be in the most dramatic place possible, and well…"

"Here I am on the roof."

"You aren't about to Hannah Baker yourself, are you?"

"Funny. Nah, fam. Just homesick."

"But you're from Jersey."

"Yeah, I'm talking about Jersey, not Brooklyn, I think."

"Cool, cool just checking. What do you miss?"

"That's the issue. I'm not homesick because I miss it, I'm sick because I'm sick of home. If anything, I'm sick of even referring to that place as home. When I leave here, I'm gonna miss this place."

Joelle didn't really know what to say after all that. I didn't expect him to. I

198

appreciated the fact he wasn't trying to force it, and was just a genuine dude. I never had a friend like Joelle or AJ, or even my grandma. Everyone back home was always so busy trying to move as fast as the world around them that they forget to just stop and breathe.

"Why do you have to leave? I thought you said you would never leave this place?" Joelle asked. I definitely remember saying that, but at the time, I was given a reason not to. I guess that's why I'm in the boat I'm in now—running away from that exact reason. It's nothing new, running away from issues instead of confronting them. Who am I to break a habit?

"No, I don't want to leave. I just feel like I have to," I answered, deflecting on the latter part of his statement. "The doctors are anticipating a good recovery with Grams and even talking about potential home attendants for her."

"That's amazing, but that doesn't mean you have to leave. You looking to go back to the city?"

"Yeah," I answered as short as I could. I didn't want to admit that everything around here reminded me of you know who.

"Well, Grams said you applied to some sort of Broadway screenwriting gig."

"Abroad," I laughed, "and yeah, I did. In a world where good things happen to me, maybe I won't have to go back home."

"Yeah, well, that's not really where we live," Joelle nudged me into laughing.

"Yeah, well, maybe I need to go back home for a bit. My mom has a spot in New York, so it will be a little change of pace. Get all this country air out of my lungs," I said, rationalizing out loud. That's when life did that funny thing she always seems to do.

"You know Brooklyn's there now, right?" Joelle's words ricocheted like a bullet off the walls around me and exploded into my face like a freshly laid egg.

"You gotta be fucking kidding me," I said as I watched the yolk drip from my forehead and into my eye.

"Yeah, bro, everybody knew that. Even Grams…"

He kept talking, but I wasn't listening. I felt like Brooklyn was haunting me now. How could she go somewhere that I had told her about? Doesn't she think everything there will remind her of me? Is that the point of her going?

Before my brain ran off the rails anymore, Joelle slapped me on the shoulder, bringing me back to reality and listening to what he was saying.

"-I just thought you should know before you went back."

"Yeah. Thanks."

"Shit, dude, come on. AJ is waiting

200

for us."

"AJ is here?"

"Yeah, you know he wanted to try this whole I'm-sick-sympathy-can-I-get-a-date-with a nurse thing he has been working on."

I felt hollow. Two of the best friends I have ever had or could ask for are here checking on my grandma and me, and all I could think about was how I wish Brooklyn were here at that very moment on the roof with me. She loved watching the lights on the poles light up against the purple and pink backdrop of the sky.

AJ and I stood up and walked across the helicopter pad to the door. When we got down to my grandma's floor, we spotted AJ walking backwards, leading my grandma by the hands.

"Very good, you two!" The nurse was cheering them on. This was a clear ploy by AJ to get her number, and it seemed to be working. AJ leaned over to my grandma and whispered something in her ear.

"Clark, you didn't Anna Baker yourself?" my grams taunted.

"It's Hannah Baker, and JoJo already used that joke."

"Awh, dude, come on, you totally stole that joke from me," AJ complained. No one could help but laugh. My grandmother could tell there were other things on my mind.

"Fuck her, Clark."

"Grandma!" I turned to see my grandma

holding up a lollipop.

"What? You too old for suckers, Clark?" she snapped.

"No, I just thought you said… never mind."

"How could you get Brooklyn from sucker?" she asked.

"He probably thought you said Fu—"

"Thaaat's enough." Joelle interrupted AJ before he embarrassed me further. "Your Grandma said we could kidnap you and get you the hell out of here, so this weekend you're all ours."

I walked AJ and Joelle into the hall and watched them hop on the elevator and leave. I walked over to the window at the end of the hall and stared out it. For a second, I thought I saw Brooklyn walk across the parking lot, but it was just my mind playing tricks on me.

Pathetic, I thought.

"What are you doing out here, Clark?"

"Grandma? What are *you* doing out here?" She walked over slowly, using her IV pole to balance herself.

"Never mind that." She paused, waiting for me to answer her question, but I didn't. "Do you know what the boys have planned for this weekend?" she continued.

"No, ma'am."

"I do. They told me."

"What is it?"

"Something you will complain about but

eventually enjoy."

"The usual, then?" Before I could even finish exhaling that sentence, grandma slapped me on the back of my head.

"What is on your mind, dear?" she asked, placing my head on her chest and rubbing the spot she just hit. I remember seeing her do this to my dad when I was younger. It felt safe.

"You ever replay conversations in your head?" I asked her. She sat silent, so I continued. "Lately, it's all I have been able to do. Sometimes I will replay it word-for-word, thinking maybe I missed something or took something out of context, or maybe I didn't read the context. Sometimes I will replay it differently, changing things I said and altering her reactions."

"You know how I love to say I told you so?"

"Yes, ma'am."

"And I haven't yet, have I?"

"This is sorta like saying it without saying it."

"Well, no. Semantically speaking, I haven't said it yet," Grams said, correcting me. "I told you everything will work out. It hasn't yet, but it will. And when it does, you'll have it written down for you to always look at and be reminded of it."

That's when I remembered one of her

'Everything works itself out in the end, and if it hasn't yet, then it's not the end.'

"You think the end will have a happy ending?" I asked her.

"Happy endings are only in massage parlors, Caleb. If you are thinking more *Thelma and Louise*-type ending, then sure, dream big."

I let the words set in, admiring my grandmother. Regardless of what her body was taking her through, her spirit and mind were incredible.

"Which sister am I?" I asked, helping her to her room. She slipped into a coughing fit in the midst of laughing at my question.

"Knock yourself out, baby. I'll be whichever is leftover," she answered, snuggling into her bed.

I keep thinking about how I should have stuck to my guns, how I should have kept my guard up, focused on writing more. Now I write to distract myself, to forget her, to forget everything. Which I guess would defeat the purpose of our experimental relationship, if it could even be called that.

I walked down the hospital hallway contemplating whether I should go back to the roof and be sad or go home and be sad. Not to jump or anything crazy like that, but for, you know, fresh air and stuff.

When I got on the elevator is when I remembered the ending to the movie *Thelma and Louise*. They were being chased by the cops and ended up in a corner. No, not a corner, it was a cliff. And they took hands and drove off of said cliff smiling and laughing.

I guess it wouldn't be Grams if she didn't leave whatever answer I was looking for up to my interpretation.

CHAPTER TWENTY

I pushed the screen door open and floated down the walkway to Joelle's car. I was in a good mood. Not because of the weed in the brownie I ate, but because they were fresh. My grandmother had some stuffed in her mailbox yesterday, and there's only one person I know who could have left them there.

Brooklyn.

The boys were suspicious of my mood but didn't say anything. I got in with the container of brownies on my lap and a bag packed with shorts, a sweatshirt and slippers because I was clueless to where we were going. I looked to the right of me and noticed all the floaties, beach towels and beer cases.

"Your laptop? Really, bro?" Joelle asked.

"Yup, got some inspiration," I said, smiling from ear to ear. "Beach? Are we going to the beach?"

AJ and Joelle answered in a mixture of 'Hell yeah' and 'Sure' before turning on the radio, which was usually on some sort of annoying rock station. When the commercial for whatever car insurance finished, an interesting melody started. The lyrics floated around the car while we all bopped our heads in an unplanned unison. The lyrics started something about not drinking coffee, only tea, and how he preferred his toast done, which instantly made me hungry. Right when the guy got to singing about being an Englishman in New York, Joelle cut the radio off and we rode in silence for a second. They were quiet, eerily quiet. AJ shook his head, trying to hold in a laugh, so I knew he was about to crack soon.

"Foreshadowing," he mumbled.

"JoJo, what's he talking about?"

"Nothing, man, I'm just talking out my ass."

"As per usual, Caleb, ignore him." AJ let out a giant laugh and turned the radio back on. And as if words from the oracle herself—my grandmother—the lyrics said something about it taking a man to suffer and then smile, so always be yourself no matter what.

The lyrics continued, this time sticking with me. Joelle cleared his throat and changed the station after seeing me in deep thought in the back seat.

"Dude, its Sting, from that old rock band The Police. Don't rack your brain too

207

hard on it," he pleaded while he adjusted his rearview mirror to me.

"JoJo, don't worry. He's high as a giraffe fart right now," AJ said, turning back to the song.

"I feel like a giraffe's ass is like human head height, so that's not that tall," I said, falling for the distraction.

"Yeah, dude, but gas rises."

"Yeah, but all gas does, so you could have said high as an ant's fart and it hold the same—wait, how could you tell I was high?"

He turned around in the seat and looked at me. I was expecting resistance from Joelle, with AJ's knees being dug into his precious seat covers, but there wasn't any. Now I was on high alert. He pointed in my lap. The container of brownies was gone. I started to hyperventilate, thinking I had eaten all the brownies.

"I think I'm gonna die. I OD'd on Brownies."

"No, we dropped those off with your grandma already. And see, I knew you were high."

"When did we do that?"

"Bro, do you have any idea what state we are even in right now?" AJ asked. I looked around, still seeing trees, and laughed.

"I literally just got in the car."

"Six hours ago," Joelle added. Like a

scene from a movie, just as he said that we passed a sign that read 'New York 97.'

"Ninety-seven miles until New York? Why are we going to New York? What's in New York?" I asked calmly. AJ slowly turned around in his seat and nudged Joelle.

"To go to the beach, bro," Joelle said under his breath.

"Driving almost eight hours to go to a beach," I said, still remaining calm.

"Not just any beach, Coney Island, bro. It's Spring break!" AJ said, as if that justified the entire trip.

We stopped in Philly for cheesesteaks, and I sat silently to listened to them explain their henchman roles in my Grandmother's devious plan.

A. Find Brooklyn

B. Get Closure

Or C. Kill Brooklyn.

I wanted to say AJ made that last part up, but knowing my grandma, she probably tried to make it step B on the list versus a plan B alternative.

"AJ, bro." I put my hand on his shoulder and laughed at them from my high horse. "Brooklyn's back home now, she's not in New York anymore. I was gonna call her after this weekend."

The two shared a look I couldn't decode. I fed the last few pieces of my sandwich to my high horse as we trotted around in our glory.

"See, JoJo, I told you maybe that's why his phone was ringing off the hook?"

"Huh? Where is my phone?" AJ pointed at the car, and I ran and snatched my phone off the charger. It was a bunch of text from my Gram's dealer, officer Robin Hood. The brownies were from him. He didn't know Grandma was in the hospital until after he'd dropped them off in the mailbox, and wanted to make sure she got them before somebody else did.

I was immediately sober after reading those last few messages. I felt alone again. Even my horse that must have manifested from the weed had left me standing under a cloud of reality with cheesesteak pieces all over my shoes. I loved these shoes. I tried telling myself that in a city full of millions of people, my luck wouldn't be so bad to actually find Brooklyn.

Then as it usually does, my luck got worse.

Turns out, AJ isn't just some athletic jock. He has been paying attention in his criminal investigation courses. He pulled up Brooklyn's new job, new phone number, address, and her new favorite restaurant's address right there on his phone.

"Creepy, right?" he bragged with a weird look on his face.

"Dude, you need help. We aren't going to find Brooklyn. She doesn't want to see me."

"I literally just found her."

"I wasn't speaking hypothetically; I was forbidding it."

"Right, we aren't going to just find her, we are going to enjoy our spring break and see her in the process," Joelle finally added to the conversation after stuffing the last few bites of his sandwich in his mouth.

"Dude, I packed juice boxes. Like tons of them. Let's just get in the car and have a couple and—" AJ said.

"What the hell are juice boxes supposed to do?" I cut him off.

"Nobody has ever been upset drinking a juice box. Besides, shouldn't you be the one that doesn't want to see her, anyway? Considering…"

"Considering what, AJ? Don't trail off, say it."

"Considering the breakup. It was pretty ba—"

"Blindsiding? Shocking? Uncalled for? Stupid? Yeah, I was there."

"I started with Ba, and none of the words you listed started wit—"

"It doesn't matter," I interrupted him again, awkwardly kicking off the green pepper stuck to the top of my shoe. He extended a juice box over to me slowly. I tried to snatch it from him, but he held on to it, pulling himself in with a hug.

"It will be fun," he laughed, holding me in a headlock.

"Listen guys, Hillary gave me permission to go, so we are going. We are like an hour or so away. And your grandma pulls rank in this situation so we might as well enjoy it."

I sat up front, because the brownie, cheesesteak and anger had started to make me carsick.

We drove mostly in silence, besides hearing AJ sigh under his breath every time he swiped left on a girl. His excuse was 'I'm passing up on so much potential.'

I felt like I was stuck in a bad movie, and in the next scene I would pull up on a horse to her favorite restaurant and she'd be there with her husband and their love child. I needed a nap.

CHAPTER TWENTY-ONE
(521mi)

"Oklahoma!" Brooklyn yelled as she perched her foot on the dashboard. She had decided to paint her nails with actual polish for a change instead of rocking whatever acrylic or oil color landed on them from painting.

"What the hell are Oklahoma plates doing all the way over here?" I laughed in confusion.

"You are staaalling," she sang as she lightly stroked the sherbet orange over her big toe.

"I just can't stop admiring you, babe. That's all."

"Awh, babe." She folded her leg in to reach up and kiss me on the cheek. "But still, as sweet as that was, I'm gonna disqualify you. Name." She finished by adjusting herself comfortably back into painting position.

"Fine, fine. If I was from Oakland…" I ended on a whisper.

"Oklahoma," she corrected. I laughed.

"Right. Oklahoma. My name would be..."

213

I paused for a moment to think of a good one. "Richard Fork and my friends would call me Pitchfork. For work I'd be… a farmer. A wheat farmer! With two wives and-"

"Whoa there, Pitchy," she interrupted.

"You are just jealous. It's better than Jorja with a J from Georgia in the A."

"Whatever, my name is way more fun, but it's fine. Your name is fine, and job is fine. Which category does the two wives fall under?"

"Well, that would fall under hardships. Being married to one woman is hell on its own; imagine two." I laughed, relieved she was equally amused.

"I'll allow it. But I'm making both wives Geminis."

"I'd rather have a micro-penis."

"We aren't mentioning existing real-life things, Caleb," she laughed. I swerved purposely, making her miss a part of her middle toe and get paint on her foot.

Brooklyn laughed menacingly and looked at me. She slowly lifted her leg over towards me and started stepping on my shoulder. I pulled over on the side of the road, and she ran crawling over the armrest to the back seat to hide. I got out of the driver seat and opened the door to the back seat. She yelled and laughed as we kissed and play-fought, getting whatever paint that wasn't dry on her toes all over the seats.

(423 Miles to Destination)

Today, a movie came out by one of my favorite indie movie studios and I can't see it. Not out in the movie theaters, but on my Fire Stick. I wanted to sit at my desk and study this movie all weekend, but I can't.

Which has led me to this question I've been trying to wrap my head around all day. Who would guess that someone who always says she's from "nowhere" when asked, would be invited so many places? Which inevitably means me as her boyfriend is invited so many places. I shook my head and laughed to myself.

"What's so funny, babe?" Brooklyn yawned, stretching out as much as she could in the passenger seat. I don't remember when she started calling me that, but I liked it. Every time I hear her call me babe or anything, it's like I'm hearing it for the first time.

"I just had a funny thought about you, is all."

"I thought you were gonna say something sweet like 'you look so peaceful when you're sleeping.' Instead, you're making fun of me," she whined while wrapping herself around my arm on the center console.

"With that snoring?" I laughed. She

215

bit me, trying not to laugh herself. I
swerved the car playfully as she screamed.

These drives were "our thing" now. I
dreaded the drive to the destination, but
usually enjoyed the drive back with her.
She was the one in charge of booking the
rental car so we could take these little
adventures. Several arguments about how I
should drive, two baby showers and one
engagement party later, and here we are.

These events always made her so
nervous and moody, which usually meant I
was on the receiving end of everything.

"What's on your mind?" she asked
sleepily. I debated answering that
truthfully. This ride had been going
smoothly thus far, and I didn't want to get
into something with her over something
little. It was always something little. I
smiled and rubbed her hand, dismissing the
question.

"I just saw Georgia plates and thought
about Jorja."

"Huh?"

"You know, like the little game we
used to play… with the license plates all
the time."

"Ohhh," she exaggerated.

"You don't remember." I shrugged her
off of me.

"No, no, I do," she pleaded.

"You know, back when we used to have
fun."

"Fuck you. I just don't remember every little thing. We are always doing little cute things like that."

"Okay, then, a Nevada plate just passed us. Go," I challenged her.

I wanted her to prove me wrong, that I wasn't just holding on too much to the little things. She sat up and looked out the window, thinking. That's when I felt the energy in the air shift. Before I could say anything, she answered with, "You'd rather be watching that stupid movie, wouldn't you?"

And somehow, in a mere second of silence, I've started an argument. "I didn't say that."

"But you didn't not say it."

"So that means attack me?"

"Why is me asking you questions attacking you? You are so guarded."

She let go of my arm and sat up to lean against her window. I didn't respond. She can continue to argue with herself if she wanted to. I am guarded, but isn't she too? If not, why wouldn't she be?

And conveniently at that moment, steam started rising up from the hood of the car. I pulled over slowly as I tried to ignore Brooklyn going into full worry mode beside me.

"Caleb! Unlock the door, Caleb. The car is going to explode, Caleb, we have to get out of the car!" she panicked, fumbling with the door handle.

"Easy, Brooklyn, easy," I said, trying to mask my   laughter. She jumped out before I could fully bring the car to a stop. "Brooklyn!" I called after her.

She was walking in the opposite direction of the car. I got out to follow her to make sure she was okay.

"What the hell is there to smirk about at a time like this?" she said, flustered.

"It's freezing out here. Get back in the car, this isn't a movie, it's not like it's going to bl—"

"Oh, you thinking something isn't a movie is rich. What are we going to do about the party?"

She plopped down on the ground in defeat. I sat down beside her as we both watch the plume of smoke slowly tire itself out.

"Everything is going to be fine, but we need to head back to the car. You don't have a jacket."

"No, everything isn't going to be fine, Caleb."

"Yeah, it is. I pressed the OnStar button before I came over. We should be hearing from somebody in like a few minutes."

"No, we won't."

"What do you mean? That happens in the movies all the time. You just hit the littl—"

"I opted out of the OnStar service to save money," she mumbled, as if that would make it less of a reality. I wanted to ask why, but she again answered before I could ask. "I needed paint supplies for the party, and was short, so—"

"Wait, whose party is it this time?"

"Sherri's bridal shower. Wait, I think it's Paige's engagement party."

"And my point has been made," I said, standing to dust myself off.

"And what point was that?" she asked, but I ignored her. I walked to the front of the car, hearing her footsteps following close behind me.

"Hello?" she continued. She tapped her foot while staring a hole in the side of my head.

"You get all worked up and thin yourself out for people you don't even know," I said, sticking my head under the hood of the car, trying to look like I knew what I'm doing.

"I know these people, Caleb. And this is a part of me growing my business, making a name for myself. Not like the make-believe life you live, wanna-be Dawson Leery."

"You spent two, maybe three months with these people. You moved around most of your life—it's like you are the most popular homeless person. These people don't remember you, they see your ads on Facebook and ask you for discounts to paint at their party. They don't even give you enough to cover the materials and the gas to get to these places. Those aren't friends."

"I've known you two or three months, does that mean I don't actually know you?"

"I don't know, Brooklyn, do you know me? Or am I just someone you slow dance with, make out with, take couples' pictures with, but introduce as your friend?"

"You know if you weren't pretending to be my boyfriend, you wouldn't be here."

"Who said I was still pretending!" I shouted, right before I felt a sharp pain on my head and started to see stars.

I felt myself falling backwards, but before I hit the ground, I blacked out.

CHAPTER TWENTY-TWO

(38mi)

"Boom! Perfect, bro!" AJ said, holding the phone up to the front seat so Joelle and I could both see.

"Nice, she's cute."

"Glad you think so. You are meeting her tomorrow morning for brunch."

"Get the hell out of here," Joelle laughed. "See, you've already got a plan B."

"He's joking, JoJo. He even said he was passing up on good potentials. I didn't understand why you didn't just swipe right on them."

"Oh, you are wrong, bro. I've swiped right on every single girl that has come across my screen for you. The potentials I would be losing out on is if they actually swipe right on you, which is the goal, obviously."

"Dude, are you serious?" I took the phone and clicked the grey profile icon and there I was. I had a Tinder Plus profile:

Caleb, 23

Screenwriter / YouTuber

Bio: The only thing lower than my standards is my self-esteem. I'm 5 foot 9 inches. (Those are 2 measurements)

"Hell of a guy"   "Outstanding Gentlemen"
  - New York Times   - Washington Post

"I wish I could be more like him."
  - The most popular kid in my high school

"He's my phone's background."   "My Hero."
  - Grandma   - Deadpool

    I thought the only up-side to the profile was the fact that he actually used good screenshots from my Instagram, until I got to the end.

    "Dude, how the hell do I delete this gif of me at the end?"

    "What? No, dude, the gif stays. What if your dance moves made her swipe right?" AJ refused. He took the phone out of my hand and sat back in his seat.

    "I'm not dancing, bro. I was petting a horse. The weed made me think I was ri… whatever." I felt defeated. I wanted so bad to laugh, but I was too much in shock at the entire situation. Maybe she only looked at the first two pictures and decided to swipe on me. Maybe she didn't even read my bio, nobody reads bios anymore. Maybe she swiped right on me by accident.

"OMG," AJ said in his most ditsy of voices, "your Bio is so funny."

"All that writing finally paid off," Joelle erupted with a cackle, joining AJ in his laughing fit. I couldn't fight it any longer and joined in with them. The worse part about the bio is I would have come up with something extremely similar, and they knew it. It felt good to have people know you better than you know yourself. It's like the great scholar Aubrey Graham said, "You only live once."

And it felt good to live again in that moment. Moments I wouldn't trade for the world.

I directed the guys to my dad's apartment in Flatbush, Brooklyn, only to find out my mom was staying there to water the plants while my dad was on a "business trip." Said business trips in the past used to send my mother into a whirlwind of emotions, assuming that's when he cheated on her. She would contemplate cheating back while he was away, but would feel horrible if he actually wasn't cheating. All of this I knew from conversations my mother would have on the phone with various girlfriends of hers. I didn't miss that.

Especially now, when things seemingly were better between her and my dad and my love life was in even more shambles than when I last lived here.

Twenty minutes after introductions, my mother texted me to ask if AJ was gay. Before I could reply no, she went on about his bravado and how super flirtatious he was. Although my gaydar was bad, I could tell this was just my mom's way of accepting rejection, assuming AJ just wasn't into women. Or maybe I was wrong.

After I showered, I came out to Joelle comfortable on the couch on FaceTime with Hillary while my mom cracked a bottle of red wine and started this weird Stifler's mom routine with AJ. They were right at home, as friends should feel in your house. I pushed my date up with Tinder girl from tomorrow morning to tonight. I was bummed about not seeing Brooklyn today, and also very relieved I didn't at the same time. I needed this distraction.

I walked down a few blocks to get to Flatbush Avenue, admiring all the things I missed about the city. I waved the Dollar van down and sat in the front seat, then held on for dear life as the driver weaved in and out of traffic like a madman.

I got off at the Barclays center, ran under the coppered-colored arena landing to beat traffic, and crossed Atlantic Avenue. I walked until I was finally at Habana Outpost on Fulton Street. This was one of my favorite places to get a Cubano sandwich, and this was my perfect excuse to come here and eat.

224

I walked through the doors to see my date nervously double-fisting two frozen margaritas. We immediately recognized each other.

"I'm sorry," she said. "I got nervous about meeting you, so I wanted to get here early and order a drink. And then I didn't know if you would come and see me in the middle of a drink, so I ordered two, and well, hi." Her spirit made me smile.

"Hi, I'm C," I said stupidly. "I'm not actually C, it's Caleb. Obviously you know that. Nobody calls me C."

We laughed as she handed me one of the drinks. We ordered actual food and then found a spot outside in their courtyard to eat. Her name was Christina. She was originally from Seattle, but got an offer to intern at one of her parents' college friend's therapy offices in SoHo at some loft building. I wanted to ask if it was Irish-owned, since Grams had always talked about how small the world was.

The night was going smoothly until she pointed out the mural on the side of the building. I forgot this place commissioned an artist every few months or so to do something new, and I was eager to see what it was. I turned to really look for the first time at the painting, and recognized it all too well.

"It's like the artist was doing puzzle pieces of the sky, symbolizing her

225

confusion and place in the universe. Even with her take of the square sun in the corner and the stars being visible while the sun is out. It's just so abstract." Cristina said.

"Small world, indeed," I mumbled.

"Come again?"

"Interesting take," I said, correcting myself.

"You disagree? Come on, tell me what you see," she begged, touching my forearm.

"I'm not nearly drunk enough—" Before I could finish, Christina got up and went inside to order more of what I later found out to be a pitcher of sangria.

One empty pitcher and six tacos later, we were feeling nice. I found myself laid out on the bench of the picnic table as she gave me her best therapy questions. It was a great exchange, until the mural came up again. She pointed out how uncomfortable I had been earlier when she mentioned it.

I sat up and turned my back to Christina as I faced this thing. "This artist is painting from the artist's memory. Something they've seen before. That's a sort of window they're looking out at, and that sun isn't the sun, it's a heater. She's in a garage looking up at what will be an apparently unforgettable memory one day."

"You said she," Christina replied.

"Huh?"

"You said they, like any gender, and then landed on she for the rest of your really good analysis of this painting. Do you know the artist?"

"You can say that."

"I think you are right. She must have painted this before in a studio, maybe looking out through a window, and then wanted to bring it here so it would be more expansive."

I didn't respond, only poured the already empty drink pitcher upside down, shaking the last few drops out. Christina touched my hand again and asked softly, "Are you okay?" She slurred her words.

"Peachy."

"Okaaaay," she dragged on. I interrupted before she could continue.

"I hate when you tell somebody about a place and then they turn that place into their place, trying to poach it from you."

"Do you think you have possession issues?"

I paused to process the question. "Huh?"

"I asked if you maybe have possession or territory issues?"

"Are you therapizing me?"

"One, that's not a word and, two, no. I'm just asking you if you feel like—"

"No, I don't feel like that. No, I don't feel— You know what, this isn't working."

227

"No, I was honestly only asking-"

"No, it's fine. You're not even named after a city."

We stopped talking over each other as a woman came over to collect our empty dishes, glasses and trash. We stood up in silence and walked outside.

"So, I'm sorry about that," I said.

"What was the named after a city thing?"

"It's nothing, honestly," I said, flagging down a yellow cab. I gave her $10, assuming it shouldn't cost more than that to get her from here to Park Slope. I went to hug her and landed on a facepalm as she snatched the money from my hand and stalked away.

I turned to try and run back into the restaurant to get a better look at that mural again, but the woman wasn't having it. I walked alongside the fence and peeked in between the holes. There was no signature on the mural, but those brush marks were familiar. The woman that denied my re-entry stopped when she saw me-half scaling the fence to get a better look. I jumped down and dusted myself off.

The woman rolled her eyes and walked past me.

"Excuse me!" I called out. She turned around and dramatically removed her earbud with another eye roll.

"I'm sorry, do you know who painted this mural?"

"Some local girl."

"Local like New York or local like…"

"Brooklyn!"

CHAPTER TWENTY-THREE

(**423mi**)

You ever wake up and not remember where you are or what time it is? I woke up and couldn't remember what planet I was on. My head was throbbing, and although I thought it was daytime, the sun was missing.

I sat up to look around and saw the rental car. That's when I remembered the radiator cap sucker-punching me. As my eyes started to focus, I saw something crouched over the hood of the open car. I jumped up, assuming it was a bear. But before my adrenaline set in, I saw it was Brooklyn.

"Caleb, close your eyes!"

"What are you doing?" I laughed.

"Whatever. It's not like you haven't watched me pee before."

"You are peeing into the radiator?"

"Unfortunately mostly on, but some in. I figured if we just got some liquid in it we could get it to a gas station or motel." I stared at her in awe, speechless.

She jumped down from squatting over the car and fixed her knit wool dress.

230

"Come on, pop those bad boys off and give this thang a golden shower. But try to aim it better than I did."

We laughed. She went and sat in the driver seat as I did as I was told. Lucky for her I had been holding it since we left, and lucky for me I didn't un-hold it in my sleep.

I looked around for the cap and screwed it back into place, then shut the hood and gave Brooklyn a thumbs up. She closed her eyes and turned the key. The car turned over like normal as we both watched and waited to see if any smoke would appear. We celebrated as none did. I jumped in the passenger seat and Brooklyn sped off.

We tried turning off of whatever side-road of a side-road we were on, but it felt like we continued to go deeper into the maze of back roads. We drove for about ten or so miles in an awkward silence that I couldn't quite figure out why it was there. Her face read like she had one hundred things to say to me but didn't know how to say them.

Before I could ask what was wrong— "Shit!" she said.

"What?" I asked. She pointed at the front of the car as the smoke started to rise again. She pulled over into a field where we sat, in more silence. I assumed the silence was equally as deafening to her as it was to me, because she clicked the radio on to whatever local broadcast was being picked up from a high school game nearby.

"Guess we are sleeping here tonight," she said, getting out of the car. She went in the trunk and got the blankets she had laid me down on earlier when I was knocked out. She got in the back seat and wrapped herself up in the covers.

"Brooklyn, it's about twenty-six degrees and only going to get colder the later it gets."

She nodded and agreed with me as we gathered what we needed and bundled up as much as we could to walk back a mile or two where there was a gas station. Our original plan: call a tow truck from there to take us to the car and then take us to the car rental place. I fought the urge to bring up how the phone charger she grabbed had a short in it, but I didn't. I've learned from watching my parents that bringing up little things like that in moments like this never helped. I doubt either of us would have had a signal had they been on, anyway.

However, the owner of the gas station informed us that he owned the nearest tow shop for twenty miles, and insisted he would help us in the morning. After assuming tonight was the night we would get murdered, since he offered us a bed in the back of his 24-hour, in-the-middle-of-nowhere-gas station/home (which Brooklyn immediately agreed to), I only wished I could have written this into a screenplay first.

We walked past the expired Little Debbie cakes aisle and the public bathroom with the out of order sign on it to the garage. There was one cruiser motorcycle there, covered in a tarp, and an old-school tow truck like the hillbilly one from that movie *Cars*. Our bed was a unique, California King futon that pulled out under the partial glass ceiling. The back wall was a roll-up door made of glass paneling, giving the room an indoor/outdoor feel. Besides the smell of motor oil and the lack of proper insulation, this place wasn't half bad.

Gas Station Morty, as he told us to call him, came in the back and told us about this rare condition where he didn't sleep, literally. Because of said condition is why his business was so successful, and if we needed him just to call on a walkie-talkie over on his toolbox. He also told us the bathroom worked fine, he just didn't want anyone else using it besides him and his cousin, who lived upstairs. Then he flicked a switch, turning on an industrial heater that faced us from across the room.

The neon orange light heated up the room quickly, and also help amplify the

motor oil smell. The hum from the heater
drowned out the bluegrass from whatever
Georgia peach radio station was playing in
the store. He held a set of keys up in his
hands connected to a melon-sized garden
gnome.

I walked over and grabbed them, then
locked the door after he closed it behind
him. I turned to find Brooklyn placing some
Glade scented cones around the floor of the
bed where were sleeping. She then revealed
two phone chargers from her purse still in
the packages. She saw the look on my face
and countered it with a look of her own
that she would obviously pay for them in
the morning. Brooklyn and I laid out
blankets over the mattress and climbed on
the lumpy, but oddly comfortable, mattress.

The sky looked expansive tonight.
There were no clouds in sight, only the
stars arranged in unknown constellations
and what seemed to be a phase shy of a full
moon.

"I'm sorry I didn't say anything back
earlier when you said that you weren't pre—
"

"No, no, it's fine. You didn't have
time before I was knocked ou—"

"Yeah, but still, I didn't know.
Didn't know you would feel lik—"

"I think I was writing a scene in my
head where the guy says that to the girl,
so don't wo—"

234

"Don't do that, Caleb," she said forcing us to finally stop talking over each other. She rolled over to look at me. "Be honest with me."

We looked at each other, listening to the hum of the heater while the air filled with anticipation of what we wanted to say.

"Look," I said, before taking a deep breath. I shut my eyes tight and exhaled whatever was on my half thawed-out heart. "I don't know when I stopped pretending we were dating, or if I ever pretended. I really do like you."

"I really like you too, which makes this all way too funny," she said, rolling away from me to lay on her back and look up at the stars.

"What's so funny?"

"I've been starting to feel all these feelings for you. And it scares me, because you are gonna go off and become this major filmmaker and I'm going to be left, heartbroken and just thinking how maybe you were right about relationships."

I rolled over to look up at the stars too. I was having an out of body experience. From somewhere far above, I watched Brooklyn and me lay together, both too nervous to look at the other.

"But what if I'm not," I bargained. Brooklyn shifted herself to face me again. I stayed frozen.

"I read some of your screenplay you

235

have been working on," she said. I felt my astroprojection crash-land on the roof of the tow truck. I watched her pull my shoulder so that we were now facing each other.

"I picked it up, flipped through, stopped on a random page, put my finger on a random line and read:

'People are attracted to things they shouldn't be. Sometimes it's like the worse something is for your health, the more you want to be around it or do it or whatever. For me it's…'

"I stopped there," she said.

"You stopped reading?"

"Well, yeah, because I didn't want to read more and find out that I was that bad thing for you that you were attracted to."

"It's fictional. It's not based on anything. You and I are—"

She kissed me. A kiss that she knew would silence me and everything else around us. We had started to open up to each other like we did when we first started talking, and I couldn't figure out why she was stopping it from happening now.

"I know," she said, before she kissed me again, this time longer and with more passion. We looked at each other for what could have been ten seconds or ten minutes. Then she snuggled into me and intertwined our legs.

"So, should we stop this?"

"I don't want to," she said, kissing me on my neck.

"I don't mean just this. This moment now. I mean everyth—"

She put her fingers over my lips and shushed me, then shook her head no as she climbed on top of me. We kissed slowly and deeply, while the moment intensified with every exchange. We have had heated conversations before, but never like the one we had just had. We've kissed thousands of times before, but it was never anything like this. Although it's been a while, we had had sex before, too, but this moment seemed different.

"Do you have protection?" Brooklyn exhaled.

"Yeah, my bag," I replied in between kisses. She stopped and looked down at me with a grin.

"And what were you assuming for this trip?" she laughed.

"Better to have one and not need one, than to need one and not have one."

"So you brought a gun?" she joked.

"Even better," I said, reaching in my bag. I pulled out a Duel Monsters trap card I had found the other day. "With this, I lay my card facedown and end my turn."

"Protection," she laughed historically. "True to your high school self. Such a nerd," she added before undoing my belt.

"You knew the reference too, fam, so fight me," I replied, pulling off her shirt. I lifted her up in my arms and slowly laid her down on her back. I climbed on top of her and swiped the hair from her eyes to reveal something in them that she wasn't telling me. I guess it was fair. I was holding on to something I've wanted to say to her for a while now. Something I had yet to say to anybody before. She could read it, though. She nodded and smiled, wrapping her arms around my head, and pulled me into her as she exhaled out.

The next morning, Gas Station Morty drove us to the car and gave us two jugs of antifreeze after we told him what we thought the issue was. I went to throw our things in the trunk, when I saw two jugs of water amongst Brooklyn's supply bags for the party.

I stood trying to process what that meant. She had to have known the water was in the trunk; did she not want to go to the gig? Did Brooklyn want us to spend a night alone together? Maybe that's what I was reading in her eyes last night, and what even was last night?

Maybe I was overanalyzing it.

Morty started the car and gave Brooklyn very complex, turn-by-turn directions to civilization. Brooklyn came to the back, where I was standing still puzzled, and casually tossed her bag in the trunk. We both pretended not to notice the elephant in the trunk.

Or maybe she purely forgot and I was still just overanalyzing. I decided to let it go.

We agreed to drive to the nearest car rental to exchange vehicles so we could make it home. Once we got in an area with service, Brooklyn made a call that changed the atmosphere in the car, again.

She hung up the phone and sat silently, but her body language screamed frustration. The moment I went to open my mouth to ask what was wrong, she put her hand over mine. Although she didn't turn to me, I could feel that whatever I was going to say wouldn't have been as helpful as this.

"Music?" I asked.

"Yes, please."

"Your playlist?" I asked again, hoping I wasn't complicating the simplicity of what was now. She thought for a moment, and then shifted herself more comfortably in the seat.

"Your playlist. Play something to match the sky."

Because I was driving, I was obviously looking at the sky. But now I was really paying attention to it.

The sun was gone, hidden behind deep, grayish white blankets. I played Sade's "The Sweetest Taboo," a song my mom used to

play and make my dad dance with her when he
was in a 'bad mood,' as she called it.

Brooklyn took up my hand and
interlocked our fingers. I pulled it to my
lips and kissed it as we drove.

CHAPTER TWENTY-FOUR
(**31mi**)

"Caleb slammed the car door and stood motionless in place. The world around him felt so real. The wind blew through his windbreaker, bringing the smell of hot dogs and cotton candy, which reminded him how hungry he was. The hair on his arms stood up as the adrenaline pumping through his body rushed from his head to his toes.

He could feel the water slowly seeping into his Converses, not noticing until then that he had stepped in a puddle. He looked down at the puddle and saw a plane slowly fly over his own blurry reflection, leaving a white line across the peach and yellow evening sky.

The streetlights slowly started to blink on one by one down the boardwalk, giving off a soft synchronized hum.

He could feel the electricity in the air and taste the sea salt as he took a cartoon-like gulp before taking this step. The step that would change his life forever.

Okay, maybe it wouldn't change his

241

life forever, but it damn sure would be a memory that he would never forget…"

I could hear JoJo and AJ snickering at me from the car.

"Is he monologuing again?"

"Yeah, I think so. Just fucking go in already!" AJ yelled.

Their words brought me back into the moment. "Get out of your own head," I told myself.

Funny, because I felt like my life flashed before my eyes as I walked to the door. I started to utter the words of the first astronauts on the moon.

That's when I pictured Brooklyn laughing. She was wearing my favorite Super Mario hoody, with no pants. Her sleep attire whenever she stayed over. I remembered her laughing so hard at me when I told her I didn't believe the moon landing was real, or even the moon, that chocolate milk came out her nose.

Brooklyn.

Reality set in again and I was halfway to the door. I started to think about how convenient it would be if a piano fell from the roof, and pow! No more anticipation.

Then it happened again, a flash.

Brooklyn and me watching Looney Toons while we baked together. We were usually baked ourselves when we did this routine. Laughing until our sides hurt, her spilling oil, making me slip and fall, just causing more laughing.

Every single thought that popped in my head, besides the ones that were actively reminding me how to walk and when to inhale or exhale, was about her.

Suddenly, I was at the door. The door that, when I walked through, would change my life fore—

You guys get the picture. I stood and took a deep breath, which was met with a lay on the horn from one of the guys in the car. Before I could turn and cuss them, the door to the shop opened.

My heart stopped.

There I was.

Face to face.

Face to face with some woman that definitely wasn't Brooklyn, and was pissed I was blocking her way of leaving. I've missed how impatient New Yorkers could be. She swung her shopping bag at me, hitting me on the arm as I shuffled to the side.

She mumbled something to me in Russian, but I ignored it. My attention was drawn to the inside of the gift shop now. For the few seconds the door was open, I caught a glimpse of a very familiar face.

I pushed through, entering the shop to a Mac Miller song I had recently added to a playlist Brooklyn and I shared.

Coincidence, I thought to myself, when there she was. A familiar face behind the counter, smiling at me.

An 8 x 10, black-and-white oil painting of my grandma on sale for $900. I remembered the day Brooklyn took this picture. Not because I remember every second with her… well, not all the time. It's just this picture particularly struck something in me that I'll never forget.

We had just finished going for a drive. When Grams learned that Brooklyn had taught me how to drive, it's all she ever wanted to do. They would sit in the back seat and smoke as I drove backroad after backroad. Those were good times.

I could tell in the moment they would be long-lasting memories.

(**DETOUR**)

"Ladies, we are going to miss the sunset," I nagged from the car. After no response, I lay my head on the steering wheel, causing the horn to honk.

Immediately the door flew open and I could feel eyes staring a hole at me for beeping at them. I couldn't tell if the look of death was from Grams or Brooklyn, but I wasn't about to find out.

The screen door closed again and I took a deep exhale. My phone went off—a text from Brooklyn that said 'lol,' confirming it was Grams at the door. Those two together were always more than I can handle, as if I could handle them one on one alone.

It was Friday. Grams still smoked, but

she had added B's brownies to her routine as well. I never could bring myself to call Brooklyn "B," but "B's Brownies" was the name of the edible bakery they had talked about opening up during one of our other sunset drives. When Grandma started to spend Friday evening to Monday morning in the hospitals, we would take that drive on Fridays and make it our day. Her day to get "literally super high," as Grams called it. It was her day to smoke in addition to taking the brownies.

I forgot how she convinced me of this being okay, but she did.

"Hey, Babe?" Brooklyn yelled while standing in the doorway. "Grams wanted me to ask where the Gorilla Glue was."

"Ummm, in the junk drawer in the kitchen, I think. What did you guys break?"

"I don't know," Brooklyn said, confused.

"Clark! I'm not asking about no daggon glue." Grandma fussed from deeper in the house. I facepalmed, remembering what Gorilla Glue was. I waved Brooklyn over.

"Yes, sir?" she said.

"Babe. She saw somebody talking about strains of weed on some show, and now everything is gorilla glue, any weed is gorilla glue."

"She is too cute."

"Babe, please can you just get her?" I pleaded, looking at the time.

"Kiss me first," Brooklyn bargained, leaning in through the passenger window. Before Brooklyn could pull her head back out the window, the screen door shut. I looked and saw Grams walking down the stairs smiling, cradling a Polaroid camera in one arm and pill bottle high in the air like a trophy in the other.

"Got it!" Grams said in a singsong voice as she got in the back seat of the car. Brooklyn shut the door and got in on the other side with her, and we pulled off. We took the most scenic and out-of-the-way route to the hospital, winding around corners while they sang Lady Antebellum's "American Honey." It was either that or TLC's "Creep," which when listened to high is like an eleven-minute song.

Brooklyn and Grams would sit in the back seat, sing off-key, talk about whatever popped in their heads and smoke. I usually ended the trip with a contact high, a face sore from smiling and laughing and a feeling of never wanting to let go of moments like these.

When we came up on the final hill right before the hospital, I pulled over off the side of the road. Our spot was on a piece of old plywood that sat in an unused driveway. If you backed in correctly, you would be hidden from the road but have the perfect shot of the sun right before its last call. I'm sure this spot was used by

246

younger kids for God knows what, but we were always gone before that time of night came.

Until then, this view was our hidden gem, the last stop on our sunset drive.

"What are you kiddos getting into tonight?"

"Caleb's going to come with me to a paint and sip I'm doing."

"Oh, that should be fun."

"Grams, please. It's a bachelorette party, and it's cat-themed."

"Here we go," Brooklyn moaned.

"I'm going, aren't I? Did you grab my computer from my desk? I wanted to see if I could—"

"No, Caleb, make me the bad guy even more," Brooklyn interrupted. I didn't feed into her response. I heard the loud sound of an older camera as she started snapping photos of purple sky stained with orange residue from the falling sun.

"I've always wanted to be a cat," Grams said, breaking the tension. We laughed at how high she was, how high we all were. Grams's laugh turned into a fit of coughs that reminded us of our destination. I started up the car again and began to pull back out to the road.

"Wait, Clark," Grandma said, catching her breath. "Take my selfie against the sun."

"It wouldn't be a self—" I shut up as

247

I felt them both give me the look of death.
Brooklyn snapped two or three more photos,
I put the car in drive, and pulled back on
to the road.

"I see why you paint, dear."

"Why is that?" Brooklyn asked her

"Well, these are all bad," Grams
replied with the typical no filter of a 71-
year-old.

"Grandma!" I yelled as I pulled up to
the front of the building.

"Nope. Except for this one. Sorry,
spoke too soon. I'm old, so I'm allowed to
do that," she backtracked quickly. "This is
the picture I want of me at my funeral,
Clark," she said as Brooklyn and I helped
her out the back. An attending came out
with a wheelchair to take her.

"Gotcha. Post it right on the fridge
for you," I said while kissing her on the
cheek. She laughed all the way into the
hospital and until the elevator doors
closed.

Brooklyn looked at me, confused, but
it was to be expected.

(**REROUTING**)

The base from Drake's "Jaded" brought
me back into the moment as the song began.
More evidence that this was our playlist.

This was definitely her work, too, I
thought as I looked around the shop. I
recognized paintings from pictures we
either took together or just from them

248

being local. We always joked about how we complemented each other so well. I always had an affinity for photography because of my obsession with cinematography. And she felt the same way with paintings and expressing her feelings for a moment. I took pictures, she painted them. I wrote scenes, she acted them out. If I had peanut butter, she had jelly.

Someone cleared his throat from behind the counter. I had forgotten where I was for a minute, or even the possibility that Brooklyn could have been here.

I turned around to a little boy at the register, scowling at me.

"Can I help you, mister?" he asked, suspicious of me.

"Are you the only one here?" I asked.

"What's it to ya if I am," he said, raising an eyebrow and placing both hands under the counter. I couldn't help but laugh, thinking this would be a pretty wacky way to die if this kid decided to end me.

I smiled and extended my hand.

"Hi, I'm..." I hesitated saying my name. "Never mind."

I turned around to head back through the exit when I noticed a picture over the door that stopped me in my tracks. I pulled out my cellphone and took a picture of it, then ran out the door as the kid yelled at me.

I ran down the sidewalk and got in the car. Joelle pulled off like the perfect getaway driver.

"Dude, what's happening?" AJ asked.

"She wasn't there," I said, short of breath.

"So why the hell am I racing away?" JoJo asked.

"Her boyfriend, maybe," AJ answered for me.

"No, dude, nothing happ— Wait she has a boyfriend?" I asked.

"I was suggesting. I don't know, she probably doesn't," AJ backtracked.

Joelle turned the radio to NPR blaring some headline about the benefits of pineapple on pizza. I picked up my phone from the seat and swiped until I got to the photo I had just taken.

It was a cartoon of *Rick and Morty*, in a gas station that looked all too familiar. Rick was passed out on the floor near the beer case, classic Rick, while Morty was just sitting on the counter with a hat that read My Station.

CHAPTER TWENTY-FIVE

"I'm gonna kill you!" she growled
angrily through her teeth. She tightened
her grip around my neck as she sat
straddled over my chest. Her smile grew
more and more menacing as I stared up at
her.

"…" I couldn't speak. I was helpless.

"I hate you," she continued. "I'm
gonna fucking kill you." She chuckled from
frustration. I gasped for air, still not
able to talk from laughing. You know that
laugh you do when you're laughing so hard
you can't do anything but try to catch your
breath? I was that kind of helpless.

"Okay, okay," I pleaded, trying more
than anything to mask the tantrum of
laughter that was seconds from erupting
again. She smiled and kissed me, still
holding what she thought was a firm grip on
me.

"Are you gonna stop laughing?" she
asked, completely flushed and out of
breath. I nodded my head yes in silence
while my smile forced itself from ear to

ear, rekindling her murderous intent. I quickly moved my fingers above her waist, tickling her and causing her to yelp out in laughter.

I shifted my weight, and in seconds I was on top of her.

(**REROUTING**)

(**22 Miles to Destination**)

"Caleb!" Joelle yelled.

"JoJo!" I yelled back, not knowing why he was calling my name.

"AJ!" AJ mumbled his own name, not to be left out. I looked around and realized we were at another one of the locations AJ said Brooklyn had been tagged under by friends on Facebook. I looked at the post AJ was showing me. It was from five weeks ago.

"Dude, she's not gonna be here," I said, sitting back further into the seat.

"I'm more interested in where you were at this point," Joelle said, as if he was catching me red-handed. I hesitated admitting my trip down memory lane was triggered by him complaining about Hillary's snoring. Brooklyn had gotten so embarrassed when I told her she snores and repeated things she talked about in her sleep.

Before the silence got too suspicious, AJ jumped in.

"That girl from last niiiight," AJ went on, "what base did you get to?"

"No bases."

"He struck out, AJ."

"I didn't strike out."

"Foul balls, then?" AJ asked.

"There was no baseball or anything last night. Only blue balls," I said. We sat in the car laughing as I got a call from a familiar looking number. I ignored it and let it go to voice mail.

"Dude, that could be the Tinder girl for tonight! Pick it up!"

"Yeah, Caleb. I think you should just get ready for the date tonight. I don't like all this Brooklyn stuff," Joelle said.

"I don't know, bro, I kind of like the pace of the city. Did you know you are ten times more likely to get bitten by a New Yorker than a shark?" We both stared at AJ, amazed at the information he managed to retain.

"I don't think that's what he meant, AJ."

"No, dude, I just think it's a bit Gosling/Dahmer," Joelle said, putting my dad's address back into the maps on his phone. I reached forward into the front seat and locked Joelle's phone screen to politely get his attention.

"You can't say something like Dahmer and whoever the hell else and not explain further," I said, extremely intrigued. AJ put his hand up to Joelle's face so he wouldn't say anything and turned to me.

253

"If the girl is into you, then a big romantic gesture works: like Ryan Gosling writing a letter to a girl every day for a year and then threatening to kill himself if she didn't go out with him. Like in *The Notebook*. But if she isn't into you, the same gesture comes off serial-killer crazy: Dahmer," AJ explained, and turned back around in his seat.

"In your case, more of a famous stalker."

"Too bad there are no famous stalkers," I argued.

"Wrong. There's Tom," he answered.

"Tom?"

"Yeah. Peeping Tom. That's stalking, too." We laughed.

"I'm not stalking anyone, so it doesn't matter."

"Not stalking if she still loves you."

"She probably doesn't, bro," I said, watching the words float out the window into the breeze. If she ever did.

The question of What is Love started to blossom in my head. I shook the thought by trying to prepare myself for Tinder date number two tonight. Last night lingered in my mouth like a bad aftertaste. So much truth I wasn't ready to face in a setting I definitely wasn't expecting it to happen in. Therapy is therapy, I guess, even if I feel like she had been scripted by my grandma to give me the gems she hasn't been able to.

That thought made me want to check on her.

I called the hospital and spoke to one of the nurses, Sonya. I was caught a little off guard by her answering because of the last time we had seen each other. Sonya Gopal was a beautiful woman. Long black hair, blue thick-frame hipster glasses, scrubs that fit in all the perfect places, hazel eyes, and she loved her job. My grandma had been pushing me to ask her out. Not discretely, either. I mean when both of us are in the room, she'd do it purposely:

"Caleb, she has a good-paying job. If you don't want to ask her out, ask her to ask you out," kind of thing.

We exchanged "Hellos" and "How have you beens" and got right to business. Grams was asleep. Sonya was on break, and like many of the other staff, they enjoyed my grandmother's company so much they took breaks in her room. Also because of this, most of the nurses there knew all of my business, sometimes better than I did.

That's why after telling me Grams's vitals had been looking strong and that she could go back to only visiting the hospital twice a week again, I wasn't surprised when she asked about my trip. The only thing I was curious about was if she knew it was to find my ex.

Though I'm not really sure what I am

255

supposed to do after I find her. What did surprise me is that she didn't know I was already on the trip and was mad I didn't say goodbye before I left. I told her I would be back soon.

I watched Joelle make wrong turn after wrong turn, and we somehow ended up at some back block with them ordering food from their first Halal truck. Because I didn't know where I was, I was growing increasingly anxious and wasn't paying attention to everything Sonya was saying about home attendants. I tuned back in towards the end when she said she would have the paperwork scanned and messaged to me via PDF.

I hung up and instructed the guys to get three plates of lamb and chicken with rice, salad and white sauce. I haven't had Halal since the last night I went to the screenwriting class, and I noticed that's where the anxiety I was feeling had come from. It wasn't the dead-end neighborhood with the abandoned cop car and stray pit bulls. It was nostalgia.

"How's Grams?" AJ asked.

"She was sleeping but is apparently ready to come home soon."

"Wait, so who was that?"

"I bet it was Sonya," AJ interrupted before I could answer. My face gave it away as soon as he said it. They busted out with laughter as I was caught in crossfire.

256

"Did she cuss you out at all?"

"Dude, it's probably not safe her working around your grandma. She could do something to her because of her probably hating you."

"AJ, too far, dude," Joelle said, throwing a punch into his arm.

"Both of you shut up. Sonya kept it professional. It's not like I left her hanging at prom. What the hell was I supposed to do?"

"Dude, you took her to the hospital cafeteria, you—"

"Yes, a place that her and I got coffee at together plenty of times." I cut Joelle off to control the narrative of his list. "I got some candles, I dressed up nice, got extra juice cups, and had gotten her favorite thing off the menu I had seen her eat every time I was there."

"You can't dress it up. You took her out to eat at her job for hospital food, and then left her with the bill," Joelle said.

"A gorgeous specimen like that, Stevens."

"After ten minutes of questions about me and Brooklyn, since she used to come with me to visit Grams, she told me she was a lesbian. What was I supposed to do?"

"Not excuse yourself to the bathroom and then go home."

"Yeah, that's sort of offensive."

257

"No! No no. I went to the bathroom and had violent diarrhea and fifteen minutes had passed. She texted me to ask if I was okay and I said I was fine. I was embarrassed. It felt like she broke up with me before I even got to my juice box. When I went back out there she was gone."

"Yeah, dating lesbians is hard as a guy," Joelle said sarcastically.

"At least it wasn't a real restaurant, and she had your extra juice box to drink. Nobody is ever not happy with a juice box, especially with two of them."

"Anyway, guys," I laughed. "Grams is good. Slower but steadier mobility, bigger appetite, little to no nausea after treatments, positive spirits." I realized that all the things on the list were probably because of the weed brownies, but was still very much happy to hear it.

When we got back to my dad's, we devoured the Halal. While I rummaged through his closet for more options besides what I packed, I could hear AJ and Joelle telling my mom how great it was to see me, as if they had driven all these miles to visit me. I didn't realize how absent I had been over the last few months until they mentioned the last time we went out together was bowling.

I think my mom was having as much fun adjusting to AJ and Joelle as I had. When I was little, my apartment or where ever we lived had been the hangout spot. Mom would make pizza rolls and give us root beer and watch us act drunk because we thought we were drinking beer beer. As I got older and more aware of my parents' relationship, I felt insecure wanting to bring friends. At least that's what I told myself. It was unfair to blame my parents for my conscious distancing myself from everyone. Sure, I learned to love my solitude. But having what I have now makes me think I had nothing at all before.

My phone rang, but it was a different number than the one I had ignored earlier. It was my date for tonight. Kassandra, with a K. Through her very thick Latina accent, she told me that she was bringing friends for my friends, and somehow we ended the conversation like Diddy at the end of that one Biggie song. We spent eight minutes alone trying to recall the name of the record to each other and another three about how our chemistries were already so much in sync.

She wasn't a therapist, she wasn't a nurse, she wasn't a stripper, and she didn't paint. Considering the encounters I've had with women recently, she seemed promising. At least promising enough that I was actually looking forward to the party tonight.

The party was like something straight out of a Hype Williams video in the 90s. It was in a four-story brownstone, every floor open to party. I found Kassandra, who preferred to just be called Sandra, with her friends and we immediately hit it off. Not too long after introductions, AJ found his way to the beer pong table and left one of the friends Sandra brought for him hanging. That left Joelle to entertain two more women than he should have been, but it was nice to see him let loose. He didn't seem too worried, and Sandra was wasting no time trying to get to know me better.

We ended up in a bathroom with a personal sized bottle of tequila she pulled from under her skirt and my hands in places I was not expecting them to be. She wanted to play a game where she would guess things about me, taking a shot if she got it wrong and me taking one when she got it right. After asking my zodiac sign, my numerical number, rising moon, and relationship with my mom, Sandra had completely abandoned the English language. She was whispering things to me in Spanish I didn't understand, but was very turned on by. We were wasted. Me partly because I didn't know the answers to anything besides zodiac, which resulted in me drinking whenever I saw fit so as to not disappoint her.

Then, typical of every New York DJ and no surprise considering the borough we were in, coming through the speakers was the legendary voice of DJ Fatman Scoop

screaming "Where Brooklyn at?" for three
minutes. It was safe to assume I had lost
all motivation, along with the excess blood
in my pants, to do anything that Sandra had
on the brain.

"Papi, relax," she said as her ice-
cold hands slid in my pants. She started to
giggle and I wanted to cry. The tequila had
completely taken over my emotions at that
point, so that's exactly what I did: cried.
Sandra was great, though. She held me in
the tub as people walked in and out to pee,
fix their makeup, or vomit in the toilet
bowl. I told her the whole Brooklyn story
and that it was in fact why I was even in
town. I even told her about finding a mural
she had potentially painted the night
before.

"So, you didn't believe in love."
"Mhm."
"And she didn't either, because she
had never experienced it?"
"Mhm."
"And you were happy, and intimate, and
you both got more out of the experience
than you expected?"
"Ehhh, yeah, I guess."
"I don't know why you guys broke up.
It sounds like you were perfect for each
other, Papi."
"Exactly!"
"But she was no good for you."
"What makes you say that?"

261

"You make me say that. You were no good for her, either. You are both liars," Sandra said, getting up from the tub.

"When did I lie?"

"You both lied to each other about what you wanted. Either that, or you are both lying to yourself or you are lying to me and I don't do liars. Even if it was only gonna be for a night."

"Wait, that's all this was gonna be? Sex?"

"Yeah," she shamelessly admitted while fixing her makeup in the mirror. I lay in the tub, still in the fetal position. Oddly, I was more turned on now than I was before. A sad boner.

"It could still be sex," I shyly suggested. She finished the last coat of red lipstick, walked over to the tub and knelt down. A guy drunkenly stumbled in the bathroom like many others had all night. This time, Kassandra screamed at him in Spanish and made him leave. She slammed the door behind him and turned her attention back to me. I was thinking maybe she had taken my suggestion into account.

"I want you all to myself right now so you can pay attention," she said, taking my face in her hands. "You have a lot of emotional baggage, honey, and I don't want you falling in love."

"I haven't been this emotional with a stranger since the last AA meeting I went

262

to," I sniffled, hugging the bottle of tequila.

"Yeah… I'm gonna go," she said, kissing me on the forehead. Sandra let go of my head and then grabbed my arm. She started writing on my arm with her lipstick what I assumed to be her address, thinking I still had a chance.

"Good luck with your alcoholism and getting over your ex. My babysitter is leaving soon. I'll just get from him what you wouldn't give me."

And then she was gone. I looked down at my arm to find a sentence in Spanish, which I was sure was different than what she had just said to me. If maybe she had spoken the words, I could have used my years of ordering food in bodegas and Spanish classes to decipher the message. But all I could recognize was the word *amor*.

Just my luck, as Kassandra walked out, AJ bust into the bathroom while I was sitting in the tub.

"Ayyyyee! Stevens, you dog! How was it?"

"Sad," I said, stumbling out of the tub.

"Awh man, you are just out of practice," AJ said, flushing and moving over to the bathroom sink.

"No, dude. I'm sad. Nothing happened." I walked over and stood in front of the toilet, realizing the only reason for my wood was because I had to go. AJ leaned against the wall and called Joelle on the phone to see where he was.

"Bro, get out," I told him.

"Dude, just piss. I'm not looking at your sad boner. No dude, he has a sad boner, not his boner is sad," he informed Joelle.

"Dude, I'm a shy pisser! Get out!" I yelled. He laughed and finally left.

I hit everything but the intended target, washed my hands and met with AJ downstairs. We found Joelle in the backyard with Sandra's friends playing giant Jenga.

"*Necesitas encontrar el amor en ti mismo antes de permitir que alguien más te ame,*" Joelle read surprisingly well off my arm.

"What the hell are you reading, JoJo?" AJ asked.

"The curse on Caleb's arm."

"It's not a curse, stupid," Joelle's opponent said, laughing at the message her friend had written on me. "It says, 'You need to find love within yourself before you can allow someone else to love you.'"

I let these words wash over me, taking them in like a refreshing drink. AJ knocked over the tower, interrupting my euphoric moment, and we left as Joelle chased him through the house out the front door.

Walking to the subway, Joelle handed

me my phone he had taken from me earlier so I wouldn't call an Uber home. I looked at my missed calls and saw one from AJ and a text from Hillary telling me I "Better not sleep with that Spanish girl." I assumed Joelle told her that's what I was doing. I looked at the missed call from the weird number from earlier and saw that they had left a voice mail. Partway through, I realized it was a familiar voice telling me they heard I was in town and wanted to see me. I smiled from ear to ear, replaying the message over and over.

"Is that Kassandra calling to thank you for an amazing ten minutes of pleasure?" Joelle asked.

"He didn't smash, bro," AJ answered for me.

"No, even better," I smiled.

CHAPTER TWENTY-SIX

(**326mi**)

"Strike! I win!"

"I've always hated how competitive you are, babe."

"Screw him, Hillary! Enjoy your victory!" I drunkenly rhymed. Hillary had turned this last match with all of us into a drinking game. For every strike somebody made, they got to set a rule for the rest of the night. Unfortunately, she was the only one to get any strikes and all her rules began with "if you are a male" and then the rest of whatever she and Brooklyn thought would be funny: flick the little man off of your cup before you drink, sentences must rhyme at all times, must agree to eat wherever the winner wanted to go to after we left bowling with no complaints.

The last rule was the deadliest, because Hillary had been on a vegan kick the past month and we were all in desperate need of real food.

I loved nights like this. Any time spent laughing and enjoying each other as much as we did is easily an unforgettable night. The guys stumbled behind the girls to the game counter where we exchanged our shoes for our debit cards we'd left on file. We walked outside and stood on the sidewalk, anticipating what tofu or salad bar nightmare awaited us.

Hillary raised her hand and announced, "Pizza Planet, dinner on me!" sending us howling with cheer as we followed behind her—all of us except Brooklyn.

"Hey, what's wrong?" I asked her. She looked down at the ground and only shook her head no.

"Hey guys, are you coming?" AJ yelled back to us. I waited for Brooklyn to answer AJ or me, but she didn't.

"Yeah man, we'll be right there. Brooklyn's feeling a little sick!" I yelled back

"I don't feel sick," she replied.

"Okay," I said, dismissing my initial thought. "Come on babe, Pizza Planet. You love that place."

"I don't want to go," she said softly.

"Okay. What would you rather us do?"

"I think I'm gonna call it a night, but you should go," she responded.

"We haven't eaten all day?" I said, confused. "Some food will make you feel better." We walked to the corner and crossed the street, following about a block behind the rest of our group. I swung my arm around Brooklyn's shoulders when she called out to Hillary. They waited for us to catch up with them at the corner.

"Hill, I'm gonna head home, I think," Brooklyn said.

"Awh girl, are you alright?" Hillary asked as they hugged goodbye.

"Yeah, I'm just tired," she replied, hugging the other guys.

"My house is closer than yours if you want to—"

"Awh, come on Stevens, you're not coming?" AJ asked. I stood staring at Brooklyn, trying to offer some answer to a question she wasn't asking but I felt she had.

"I'm gonna just go home," she said before kissing me on the cheek. "But you should go."

"Piss or get off the pot, boys," Hillary said, running across the street as the light changed. Brooklyn started walking off in the opposite direction. I whistled and waved goodbye to the group, then ran to catch up with Brooklyn.

We walked with our steps almost in unison, which was odd. My legs were longer than hers, so that meant she was walking faster than normal. I reached out for her hand, but right as my skin touched hers, she folded her arms. Maybe it was just in my head.

"You sure you are okay?"

"Yeah. I'm okay," she replied. She unfolded her arms and slowed her pace a bit and wrapped her arm in mine. I kissed her on the forehead and felt her cheek rise against my forearm. I smiled as we walked for a bit more.

"It's gonna rain," she said.

"Is it?" I looked up at the sky and didn't see a star in sight. The moon barely shined through the clouds and I noticed the smell of rain in the air. We stopped on the corner of the street my grandma's house was on. Brooklyn's face read like she wanted to tell me she was going to continue home, but before she could open her mouth, the bottom of the sky fell out.

She grabbed my hand, or I grabbed hers, and we ran to my grandma's front porch.

We got in the house and kicked off our wet shoes and left them by the door. We walked up the stairs as a flash of lightning lit the way.

"Nice cinematography," I joked. We got to the landing and I turned the light on in the bathroom. Brooklyn walked in behind me and turned the hot water on in the shower. She took off her clothes and hopped in all in one motion. I grabbed her towel out of my room along with her slippers and brought them to her.

I sat them by the sink in the bathroom and went to leave when she asked me to join her. I stripped and got in. I had never showered with anyone before. I thought it was dangerous, depending on how sudsy things got and how much your life depended on the other's grip with the bottom of the tub.

All of those thoughts quickly drained away as we stood under the water surrounded by steam. I reached for her loofah and lathered it up as the smell of lavender and almonds filled the air. I pressed it against Brooklyn's back and rubbed it from shoulder to shoulder.

She turned and faced me with mascara and eyeliner melting down her cheeks. I rinsed the loofah of all the soap and wiped the black streaks from her cheeks. She faced the showerhead and rubbed her eyes of the rest of the makeup, then reached behind me for her towel and stepped out, dripping on the floor.

"Thank you," she said, kissing me and then slipping out of the bathroom. She turned the light on in my room and I could see her shadow drying off. Then she went in the drawers of my dresser to find whatever hoodie she wanted to sleep in as per usual.

I finished up in the shower and killed the water to hear a loud boom of thunder. I walked in the room to Brooklyn facing the window, watching the rain fall. I grabbed my pajama pants off the floor from where I threw them this morning and climbed in bed behind Brooklyn. She grabbed my right hand and pulled it over her, bringing me closer. We watched the branches wave methodically in the wind.

"Glad you arranged tonight, babe. It's been a while since we went out and had THAT much fun with everyone. Like series finale fun," I thanked her.

"Caleb," she said.

"Yeah?"

"I think we should break up." Her words were like a grenade, its ringing aftershock muffling everything around me. I couldn't move. I didn't know what to say.

"I said I think we should break—"

"I know what you said. Why are you repeating it?"

"Well, you said huh," she told me, her voice holding back whatever emotion she could.

"I did? I'm sorry. I didn't think I said anything. I didn't know I could say anything. I'm sorry."

"It's okay."

"Wait. Why am I apologizing? Can you let go of my hand please?" I jerked loose from her and scooted to the edge of the bed. She turned over and faced me with glassy eyes. She looked at me, wanting to say something. I was also waiting for me to say something, I just didn't know what. She tried to touch me again and I flinched.

"I thought we were good after the gas

station night…"

"Me too."

"So what the fuc—" I erupted, falling off the bed. Not in an embarrassing adding-insult-to-injury way, but in a cool I'm-upset way. She sat up and wiped her eyes. I felt stupid standing there naked, but I couldn't act like I cared, not at that moment.

"I saw your letter from the abroad Sundance Institute. You lied and said you weren't accepted. So you didn't plan on going." Brooklyn always made me feel like a deer in headlights when she ended her questions without question marks.

"No, because I want to stay here with you and the fellas and Grams and—"

"And that's not fair," she said in a full-on cry. "You don't get to make everyone around you the reason why you don't follow your dreams. Things like this only happen once in a lifetime."

"Brooklyn, it will work itself out. I was thinking I could write and shoot some stuff myself. Like off of our lives, sorta like a modern version of *Dawson's Creek*. I'd be—"

"You'd be Dawson and I'd be Jennifer."

"Brooklyn. No, I wasn't gonna say Dawson. He didn't end up with who he wanted and Jen died."

"I know she died. See that's the thing, Caleb. Nothing is real to you.

272

Everything isn't a sitcom and I don't want to be just some role in your coming of age movie."

"What are you talking about? This is real, we were happy."

"Like pigs in shit." she said, sitting up. "In the beginning it was both of us acting, it was fun. Now here recently everything has been a full-on production for you. I don't even know who you are."

"See, now that's pig shit." I said, getting completely out of the bed.

"Do you even remember me asking about you about who you were in high school?" she sat up and leaned against my window, "You gave me a bunch of TV references. I had to wait until you were around your friends at the campfire to hear something real about your past."

"It was a joke!"

"Everything is a joke to you."

"No."

"Then what isn't?" her voice cracked. She sat with an expression I couldn't quite define. Was it anger, general confusing, hope? Maybe it was all three, but I couldn't read it, I was to blind by my own emotions.

"My work." Her façade fully broke into tears at my lie; "You always distracted me from it so we could do something you wanted to do." I wanted to shut up, "You never cared." But I couldn't stop, "So don't act like you care now, CHRIST shut up Caleb."

I wasn't sure what I was saying out loud anymore, or what was just thoughts in my head. I was hurt. I didn't mean all of these things, or maybe I did? I didn't mean to say them like that if at all.

"Caleb, said after finally composing herself, "You always wanted to do buys work. Not actual work on your own things. So I figured maybe we just haven't done enough things together to inspire you. I just wanted to inspire you."

"You are wrong. You did inspire me. And I was happy! I know, I know I said a bunch of things just now but just think. Reme-"

"Caleb." She cut me off as she crawled over to sit on the edge of the bed in front of me, "I think you are only remembering the good parts."

I went back to the weekend when Brooklyn and I had our Half Baked bake-off. Brooklyn found her dad's old DVD player and a few movies while looking for some old pictures. This spur of the moment exploration sparked an amazing throwback theme movie marathon. We split and ate half a weed cookie while we watched *Half Baked*.

At some point during the movie, Brooklyn decided since we didn't have snacks, we would bake some. She called Hillary for her grandma's cinnamon red velvet cake recipe. She told her it was for a baking competition, leaving out that she was going to add weed. Once she hung up and put on a slew of different *Cupcake Wars* and *Cake Boss* type shows, our mini competition began. Our bake-off charade slowly turned into a husband and wife bit. I didn't mind, assuming I could build on it and use it in one of my writing pieces some day in the future.

Anytime Brooklyn was at her most peaceful, she was painting.

Anytime Brooklyn was at her most vulnerable, she was baking.

Because I was already high from the cookie, I forgot this fact about her. Needless to say, when she started sharing, I didn't pay it any mind. She told me stories about her dad and how he wished he'd pursued her mom more. She said her mom divorced him and left them both because she was sick of being an army wife.

My regrettable response was telling her she should let me write her own spin-off show and produce it once I've made it big. She didn't like that one bit.

I assumed she'd made it up because one: she was high and I figured she was deep into her wife role, giving me some random backstory.

Two: she had told me her mom passed away giving birth to her.

Three: again, I was high and didn't know what I had said was bad!

She threw flour, splashed batter and frosting everywhere, and smashed whatever glass cups were drying in the dish rack. In her tantrum, she revealed to me her mother dying was just a story she told herself and everybody who asked. I apologized in my worst Gordon Ramsay impression, getting her to at least crack a smile and stop crying for a few minutes. It didn't last, though.

She slept on the couch as I cleaned up the mess. I was able to salvage a decent amount of batter and turn them into microwave mug cakes, following along with whatever episode happened to be on. The microwave went off, waking Brooklyn and bringing her into the kitchen.

Brooklyn stopped me from cleaning and kissed me as tears fell from her face. Heavy, passionate, and emotional kisses. I wanted to apologize again for what I said, but she stopped me. We ate the mug cakes, forgetting there was weed in them, and ended up sleeping through the weekend.

I thought about the carnival again. I had talked Brooklyn into getting on the Ferris wheel even though she was afraid of heights. Sad to say, we ended up stuck at the top, and Brooklyn didn't say a word the entire time. She just squeezed my hand for the thirty minutes we were up there, frozen in fear.

I tried to people-watch like I do with my Grams to lighten the mood with her. I even tried to turn the negative into a positive. I took really great pictures, suggesting she could paint them later. It didn't work.

I remember I had originally wanted to do dinner and movie that day, but Brooklyn insisted eating while we were there since it would be cheaper. It wasn't cheaper: ten dollars for an Italian sausage and fifteen for a chicken kebab that made me feel sick for the rest of the evening.

That was the same day she had promised me we would go to see the new indie movie *BLVD of BRKN DRMZ*. I was commissioned to do a review of it for the blog. I had been slacking lately, not really racking up the lengthy portfolio I was hoping to have when I applied to different studios. By the time I saw the movie, there were already four other reviews posted, and I missed out on it.

To top it off, I didn't even win her the giant teddy bear she left the carnival with. Some guy I was playing the stupid game against gave her the bear after she introduced me to him as her friend. That didn't bother me as much as it did when she exchanged social medias with him. The rest of that night I remember in a blur, besides one thought that kept poking and prodding me.

I was upset and had a right to be, while at the same time I didn't. Because we were just friends.

I thought about our countless road trips. Those were undeniable fun times. Of course, there were a few arguments while she was teaching me to drive, but that's normal for anyone. There were plenty of drives into the sunset. Maybe more than half of those she was asleep for, but still romantic nonetheless.

All little things we moved past, until the night we broke down. I remember after that, she convinced me to go with her to another wedding. She told me I would actually be her date and not just the entertainment's plus one. I gave in.

Most of the time there I spent alone, like the other events I drove her to. Watching her from across the room, being the life of the conversation. Whenever I was by her side, I introduced myself before she could call me just her friend Caleb again. It was even weird when it was time to catch the garter and bouquet. She cheered me on to catch it, gave me a pep talk and kissed me for good luck and everything. I did my best Odell Beckham impression to secure the grab, one-handed over a bunch of guys taller than me.

But when it was her turn to catch the bouquet, she ran from the group of women once the flowers were in the air.

It all started to feel like a dream. Everything that was happening, the things I was remembering, it couldn't have been real. This trip down memory lane was more like waking up. Maybe more like a nightmare as I remembered more and more.

Us chilling in a hotel after one of our mini road trips. Everything was going smoothly that day. We made it to the hotel and immediately hit the hot tub. We didn't get a chance to relax too long, though, because Brooklyn had the urge to give me swimming lessons. After a lengthy back and forth of me telling her my body doesn't float, the water was going to be too cold, and we had just eaten, she finally dropped it. She asked me to sit on the edge with her with just my feet in the water while she floated around.

It seemed simple enough to do, until she pulled me into the water. We were at the deep end, and I couldn't touch the bottom. Why a hotel with three stars should have a pool that deep beats me. But that's exactly what I feel like now.

Unexpectedly getting pulled into the deep end of the water.

Thinking maybe if I sink to the bottom, I could push back up to the surface.

These emotions were overwhelming, like waves in a storm. The bottom felt like there would be no return if I fell further. I closed my eyes and reached out for Brooklyn's hand as I had in the pool. Then,

she had taken it and swam me to the shallow
end where I could climb out and take my
breath.

This time when I reached out, I could
feel her reach back, but she was not there.
At least not to save me, not this time.

I snapped back to reality, opening my
eyes to her sitting in front of me. Her
face was drenched from tears, and it almost
made me mad seeing her heartbroken as if it
was me ending things. I sat down beside her
and put my face in my hands. She hugged me
from behind as we sat quiet for a while.

"What's wrong with only thinking about
the good?" I asked finally, ripping through
the silence.

"Nothing, if it was real.
But it wasn't.
None of it was."

CHAPTER TWENTY-SEVEN
(20mi)

I'm dreading getting out of bed today and taking this long drive. I haven't slept much since being on this road trip, so I'm excited to head back home to sleep. Funny, me referring to Grams's as home while I lay in my own room, but that's what it was.

My brain has been a bit fuzzy recently. Maybe less fuzzy and more distracted, like I can feel something coming or going to happen. I relived a lot of emotions I didn't know I needed to live again.

It's been a while since I spent time with my boys, and I got to do that again. Funny, with all my failed dates, AJ was the one to actually meet someone. Sure, that someone is a woman that went to school with my mom, but I was just happy it wasn't my mom. Mom and his flirtations were a little too intense for me for a bit, but thank God that's all it was.

Joelle ended up joining a Subaru car club to get this custom, limited-edition tint, which he's sure to get tickets for when we get back. JoJo FaceTimed Hillary every chance he got, which I thought would annoy me but was more admirable than anything. Their love was hopeful.

And I got closure. Maybe not the closure I wanted, but I got the closure I needed.

I'm glad Grams orchestrated everything the way she did. It's like I was driving as fast as I could to get away from everything at home in the city, and when I returned, I found that the things that were the end of the world to me before just weren't now.

Grams being Grams, I'm not sure her intentions were totally overt. She told the guys she wanted me to go and get closure with Brooklyn, and I'm not sure how true that was. She knew there was a Superman pop-up while I was there, and of course made me go and FaceTime her.

The only closure I got was an unexpected call from my old screenwriting mentor. I suspect Grams got the school information from Brooklyn after she saw that letter, but I guess I will never know. I wasn't expecting to see Brooklyn. With everything else from the trip being so overwhelmingly good, it didn't matter if I did or not. After a while, I started to see Brooklyn in places I went, songs I heard—I wondered if she was playing them—and accidental nostalgia trips. At first I just chalked it up to life being life, but then

out of nowhere it felt like life went too
far.

I relapsed hard on my emotions and
crashed.

I was told to write a letter to you,
to get closure since we never got a chance
to speak. Doesn't make sense to me, to
write a letter you will never read, but
whatever. I'll drop this paper in a black
hole and watch the universe go on like it
never mattered if I wrote a word down or
not.

It's been a while since that trip.
Time has been very abstract to me, so I'm
not quite sure how long it's been. I told
my mom I saw the sunset three times in one
day and she brought me here to get help.
Turns out I just wasn't sleeping and had
been up for three days.

My dad came soon after I was—I don't
want to say committed—brought there. Before
leaving, the doctors said to take all my
emotions, all my thoughts, all my writing
skills and all my time and pour it all out
to you on paper. So, here it is.

I feel like I've been detoxing from my
emotions and the reoccurring feelings of
everything. The tears, the wanting, the
depression, and even the shakes from just
being so damn angry. I do think, though,
that it is okay that I'm angry, or was
angry. At least I'm feeling something again

283

other than numb.

It's just I didn't know things were as bad as they were, no one did. You knew, though, and chose not to tell me. I know I'm doing that thing where I take other people's situations and make it about me. But I thought we were in this thing together. Of course you leaving was inevitable, I'm not that naive, but you didn't even let me say goodbye. Didn't you want to say goodbye to me?

I feel like I'm fighting for a fix of you. I'm craving for just one more of our conversations, to hear your voice, update you on my life. I'm itching for one more exchange of inside jokes, the inappropriate ones, the ones only we would get, the ones you steal from your favorite shows. I long for more time together, just one more moment of creating memories, looking back on the time spent, even planning to do things we would actually never set out to do.

I miss your love. Being with you has reminded me what it is to truly find love and lose it. Because of you, I've found love I didn't even realize I was missing in my life with AJ and Joelle. I love these guys like brothers, and that I never had before.

But this is different than the love I have for my friends.

My parents lost love for each other

and found it again in friendship. I watch them now interact, and it's almost like us. Once their confusion around what love they had for each other was gone, they found a love that works. I think it helped mend my relationship with them a lot.

Even with my work, I think you've accomplished the refrigerator thing you were looking for. I've stopped holding on to this place as a safe haven now that you are gone, and I'm moving on, thanks to you.

I've never been at a low this low before. At first I thought this was just one of your jokes. You knew how I would react and just wanted to see how far I would go.

Joke's on you. I went somewhere neither of us would have guessed.

I remember waking up and seeing the IV in my arm, realizing that I was in a hospital room. That this was real. It really sucks, but it's a part of life.

Before, I'm not sure I would have realized how fortunate I actually am. I am surrounded by friends and family who've been here to help me through this dark time without you, and I know if you could, you would be here too.

So I hug this now empty bottle of Jack "Danielle," as you called it, writing this letter and preparing myself for the final goodbye. I still can't believe you are gone. They say with time it will get better, but you know how I am with heartbreak, even though this is more of a heart shattering into dust thing.

Hell, from meeting Brooklyn to being over her took damn near 500 Days. Don't worry, I know how competitive you are, and I'm sure it will take me twice as long to get over you.

I will miss my Oracle, and I love you.

"Caleb, are you finished with your letter, honey?" my mother asked as she stormed down the hall to stand in the doorway. She stood there tapping her black heels against the wooden floor, purposely sending thunderous hangover echoes through my skull.

"Caleb," she said sternly. I moaned through the fort of pillows where I was hibernating. "Are you going to get up?"

"Mmmhmm…" I moaned again.

"Your grandmother would kill you if you were late."

I didn't have a reply this time for her. More footsteps showed up to the doorway.

"Come on, Champ," my dad said while my mom adjusted his necktie. "I left your suit upstairs in my old room."

I sat up and crawled to the edge of the bed, then placed my feet on the cold wood floor. I looked up and noticed my dad had his "Guaranteed hangover remedy" in hand. A room temperature red Gatorade and toast was his cure-all.

I walked over to them and took the plate and bottle. I haven't seen them this friendly, or even civil, in a really long time. I wanted to say something to them, but dad walked back down the hallway and out the front door.

"When's the last time you were in this house, mom?" I asked her. She shoved a piece of toast in my mouth and laughed.

"I think you were ten or so," she said, walking over to the bathroom. She turned the shower on and opened the medicine cabinet. "Your father and I had an argument and I left and came here. Spent some time with your crazy old grandma. Every reason I told her for every fight, she told me to leave him because of it."

"She told you to leave dad?"

"'That bastard! He doesn't adjust the seat in your car no matter how many times you tell him? Leave him!' is what she would say. Just pointing out how stupid everything we fought about was. It happens. We forgot that at some point." She walked out of the bathroom and dropped three Tylenols on the plate.

I walked back into the room and sat on my grandma's bed. I watched the steam from the bathroom spill into the hallway and slowly in the room towards me as I ate the other slice of toast. I chugged the

287

Gatorade and tried to imagine the room wasn't spinning as fast as a tornado.

When I opened my eyes, I was showered, dressed, and outside. I was surrounded by everyone I cared about, but was the loneliest I've felt in a long time. My parents were here together, but not together.

Joelle, Hillary, AJ, officer Robin Hood, and a few other people were all here for my grandma's "going away party" as she demanded it be called. A funeral for any normal dead person, but normal would be the furthest adjective to describe who she is. Who she was.

I was the only person there in all-black, against one of the many items on my grandmother's forbidden list. Instead of music, Jerry Seinfeld's standup bits were playing softly in the background. Not just because she wanted to pretend he would attend her funeral, but also because his jokes should keep people from crying. Crying was on the forbidden list, along with pigtails, anyone she hadn't spoken to in the last two years, selfie-sticks, Snapchat, cats, people who prefer Batman over Superman, and Jessica Bechman if for any reason Grams's childhood nemesis outlived her.

I thought the service was beautiful, the blur of what I remember of it, anyway. When they lowered her into the ground, my life for the past year and a half with her flashed in front of my eyes, blinding me with emotion. Tears stung my eyes as I tried not to break down crying and have her laugh at me from the other side.

There weren't many times I looked at my dad and admired him, but the strength he showed me today was strength inherited directly from her. Which means I had it in me, too.

That thought alone made me smile.

As the sun began to hide behind the trees, and stars started to reveal themselves one by one, people left. AJ, Jojo, Hillary, and I stood in front of her plot.

"Thanks for the party, Grams," AJ said before pouring a pill bottle of seeds into her grave.

"Was that marijuana seeds?" Hillary asked, reading my mind.

"Just following instructions, sis," he answered. I laughed. I stood up and grabbed a shovel that was sticking in the ground. We all took turns filling the hole as much as we could, only leaving whoever's job this actually was just the details to fix.

"Caleb, so when do you leave?" Joelle asked me.

"Wednesday."

"Wait, you aren't staying?" Hillary asked.

"No, I'm not."

"He was only here for his grandma, Hill," AJ added.

"Initially, yeah, but—"

"Yeah, but so much as happened since. And that's so soon. It's Monday, Caleb," Hillary interrupted, drilling me into a corner.

"A little help here, JoJo?" I laughed.

"You knew about him leaving and weren't going to tell me?" she yelled. She grabbed him, pulling her phone from his pocket and started texting dramatically.

"You literally heard me ask just ten seconds ago for the answer."

"This was both of their going away parties," AJ added.

I watched them argue back and forth while I laughed. I was going to miss this. Which reminded me.

"Hey, AJ, I thought you were supposed to give me my grandma's notes and instructions for today," I asked him.

"Yeah, I'll have them to you before you leave."

"Dude, you have them on you now. I saw you look at it all day," I questioned him.

"Jesus, Stevens, you'll have it tomorrow or something," he said, hugging me as tight as he could. I smiled and let it go. I said goodbye to everyone and sat there with my grandma. I was quiet for a long time trying to still make sense of it all. Maybe I was waiting for her spirit to come up out of nowhere and we'd have some final conversation.

But that's just my brain thinking everything is a movie again. I hate to say it, but maybe Brooklyn was right.

Even if I still don't know what's so horrible about that. Movies are great. I don't think I really live a happy ending type life, but I'd welcome it if that's how it was written. This isn't *The Truman Show,* and I have no desires to be anything close to that. This past year was great, but I'm exhausted from all the life lessons. It would be just like my grandma to give me the closure I needed to propel me into the next stage in my life.

"Grams, if it wasn't for you forcing me to go to New York, I wouldn't be where I'm at now. You were looking out for me like always, and I hope…"

I had to choke back the tears before she started to make fun of me from the other side. "And I hope you continue to. Since you passed, I got a call from the overseas company. After I went and sat with the writing school and got my actual letter of recommendation, they reached out to the program. They are changing my internship to an actual writing position."

Just as tears started to run down my face, a mosquito bit me on the cheek. All I could do was laugh.

Wouldn't be a kiss from my grandma if it was anything different.

291

CHAPTER TWENTY-EIGHT
(20mi)

I can't breathe. My ribs hurt and I'm buckled over on my knees, dying. I haven't laughed this hard since, well, the last time I laughed this hard. That's the thing about Joelle and AJ. These moments happen all the time and can happen at any moment. It took us hours longer than it should have to pack up my stuff because of it.

I could tell they were going to miss me just as much as I was gonna miss them. Because we are men, though, we can't just say that. Which sucks, but the message was clear.

If this was a TV show, we'd have a moment where the studio audience would "awwwhhh" afterward and applaud, and then we would cut to the next scene of me driving away slowly from the house.

Good thing this is reality, because that ending would have made this leaving thing a lot tougher. My mom and dad decided to pay for my ticket to Europe. The cheapest flight was three connections and left immediately, so there was no real time to wallow in any state of being besides preparation.

My parents decided to drive me to the airport. I anticipated an awkward, hour-long drive, but it wasn't. It was nostalgic. I felt like a little kid watching my parents interact with each other from the back seat. Just like back then, there was a clear tension of some sort. But unlike then, now they aren't trying to hide the fights. The bickering was in front of me, not just when they thought I wasn't listening or I wasn't around.

They were fighting about what exit to take because of which route would be quicker. The only thing that shocked me about these new exchanges is that they were followed with laughs and smiles and fun. I imagined this is what they were like when they were friends before dating. I laughed to myself. Imagine that, love ruining friendships.

"Or bringing them back together," my mom said, answering me.

"Wait, what? Was I thinking out loud?" I asked.

"No, I don't think so. I asked what did you pack for the weather?" She laughed.

"I'm not really sure where I'll be filming, or where I'll be. But I have some hoodies and t-shirts, slacks and jeans."

"No button-ups, blazers, trousers?" my

father added.

"Trousers?" I laughed. "No, dad, no trousers. Slacks, yeah."

"You are gonna have to distinguish your look from other people and other talent as a writer, Champ."

"Dad, could you not call me Champ or say Champ unless it's talking about the hoodie or something."

"I told you he hated it," my mom chimed in.

"Since when?" he asked, offended

"Since forever, dad. I'm not even athletic," I laughed. I loved seeing my parents this way, and we talked about what had happened with me since I left Jersey. But before I got to how I had gotten this job, my mother reminded me of the purposely gaping hole I left in my story.

Brooklyn.

"You came to Brooklyn to see Brooklyn. Didn't you?" she interrogated.

"Now wait. Go back and fill us in on her and how you met her," my dad said.

"No and No," I deflected.

"Fine, then I'll fill your father in on my horribly secondhand version of the story."

"Oh, so you told her and not me?"

"No, his friends did while Caleb was out on a date."

"Ayyyeee, that's my boy."

"I am not your boy," I laughed. "Mom,

294

don't. I met a girl. She was cool. Shared a lot in common besides views on relationships."

"And then got in one with her?"

"See, that is your boy," my mom jabbed.

"Mom, please. Long story a lot less long, we dated, I thought it was real, it wasn't, it ended, she left, I'm leaving." The car was silent. Deafeningly silent, almost.

"I think we are being followed," my dad said. I went to turn around in the seat and he almost had a heart attack, saying we could give away that we notice them.

"It's probably something that looks similar to something you saw before. Cars do that, you know," my mom said.

"No, I passed it leaving mom's. And now it's going the same direction we are, I bet."

Just then, the GPS on the phone said to take the next exit to the airport. We looked at each other and decided to see if my dad was right. Maybe I forgot something super important, and somebody wanted to make sure I had it before I left.

"I got pretty good at noticing tails for the few weeks your mother was having me followed."

"I just wanted to make sure you weren't doing anything you weren't supposed to. Maybe it's Brooklyn," she said to me.

295

"Not funny."

"You can't be so angry about her. She doesn't sound like she was the greatest girlfriend."

"How am I making it sound?"

"JoJo an—"

"Don't call him JoJo, mom, it's Joelle."

"JoJo, like I was saying. I can call him JoJo. He and Adrian said that since you guys broke up, you've been spending more time on your work. All of your movie reviews for whatever place were better and more entertaining. And you are actually going through with this job that you turned into a job from an intern."

"Who's Adrian?" I deflected.

"AJ."

"Awh, mom, call him AJ. I didn't even know that was his name."

"What did you think AJ was short for?"

"I don't know.

"We are here," my dad said, pulling up to the departures curb of the airport.

"So what time do you get to New York?" my mom asked, her voice suddenly filled with tears she was holding back.

"Eight o'clock. Next flight leaves at nine-thirty or something."

"So that's a nine o'clock boarding," my dad said, not taking his eyes off the rearview mirror. "You won't have time to mess around once you get your luggage and

go to the next gate," he finished his
lecture.

"Get out and hug your son. We aren't
being followed."

"Could be one of my ex-girlfriends
from high school saw me and wanted to
confess their undying love for me," he said
while I was getting out of the car. I
turned around to see who my dad could have
been talking about.

It was Brooklyn.

She was grabbing a duffle bag out of
the car. I must have been staring in shock,
because I didn't notice Brooklyn's dad
walking over to me until my dad stepped in
the way.

"Who the hell are you?" my dad asked
in a fake deep voice.

"Dad, move. He's like super-bigger
than you."

"Your mother has her gun on her.
Right?"

"The one your mom gave to me," she
replied, patting her purse.

"Sorry. I know this young gentleman.
It's been too long, Mr. Stevens," her dad
said, giving me a hug.

"Who are you hugging?" Brooklyn asked,
walking up behind him. When he let me go
and our eyes met, her expression was as
shocked as mine.

"Brooklyn," I said. She looked at me
as if she had seen a ghost. She didn't say

anything.

"Hell of a going away party you missed," I continued. Her eyes started glassing over as I walked away. My dad handed me my last bag as I kissed my mom and dad goodbye.

"Nice seeing you, Mr. Stevens!" Brooklyn's dad yelled. I smiled and waved back, then walked into the airport.

I could see my mom and dad talking with Brooklyn and her dad as I stood there just inside the airport doors. I didn't know what I was waiting for.

I realized I was having another movie moment, where maybe she'd rush in and confess something that would make all of these feelings I've been suppressing or even forgetting go away.

Frustrated with myself, I stormed off. I got in line at the ticket counter to check my bags. I paid extra to keep one as a carryon, because I didn't know if all four would make it to my final destination after three connections.

Chills shot through my body as I regretted the thought *Final Destination.*

I walked over to security to see the last person in line was Brooklyn. I waited to let an older lady in front of me so I wouldn't be directly behind her. Petty? Maybe jaded was the better word, but I didn't care.

Then a family of six came behind me,

telling me that they were with their grandmother who I let in front of me and how they wanted to stand with her. Karma, I thought to myself.

After throwing out my coconut oil because TSA is the devil, I headed to my gate. I looked at my ticket. I was group ten and boarding wasn't for another eight minutes, so I went to get some food while I waited.

I looked at the departures for the day while I was standing in line, and saw that this was the last flight out to New York. I shook my head, laughing at the thought of me getting a seat next to Brooklyn. She could be going anywhere.

I put my headphones on and started scrolling through Spotify for my Soundtrack of a Book playlist. I skipped past my favorite Smiths song because it made me think of Brooklyn. Of course, this entire playlist did, so I left it on Rihanna's song 'Never Ending.'

"Can you move up in line?" a woman said from behind me. I turned up the music and shuffled as close as I could before touching the backpack of the guy in front of me. The woman repeated herself louder.

I turned around.

It was Brooklyn. I took my headphones off and stared at her.

"I said, I put you on to that song."

"Oh, I thought you were telling me to

mov— It's fine." All the hostility I had
felt raging through me moments ago was
gone. Now I was hanging onto the silence in
the conversation like a cliff, hoping she
would pull me up.

I turned back around to not make that
fact too obviously known, then I moved up
in line trying to think of the least
awkward thing to do. I waited. I turned
down my music and left my headphones around
my neck, and waited.

I was waiting so intensely, I forgot
that I was actually waiting in line for
food. The cashier waved me forward with a
smile.

"I didn't miss the party," Brooklyn
said while the cashier greeted me.

"I'm sorry, what?" I turned to her.

"I said I didn't miss the going away
party," Brooklyn repeated.

"Sir?" the cashier called me. I
apologized and stared up at the menu. I got
a chicken sandwich and fries, then stepped
to the side as the cashier looked at
Brooklyn. Brooklyn smiled and waved that
she was fine. I stepped back and wrapped my
arm around Brooklyn's shoulder to pull her
forward with me. Everyone laughed while she
ordered a large lemonade and large fry. I
paid, and we moved out of the way and
waited.

Brooklyn pulled out a chocolate chip
cookie wrapped in Saran Wrap. I looked at

her and she smiled a guilty smile. I
laughed and mouthed no as she broke the
cookie in half. She gave me half and then
wrapped the other and placed it in her
purse.

She broke the half she gave to me and
held it in front of my face. I shook my
head no again as she started doing airplane
noises and gestures. We laughed and I caved
in and grabbed it, then wrapped it in a
napkin and placed it in my pocket.

The gate agent started an
announcement, and I noticed Brooklyn paying
attention to it also.

"Your flight?" I asked, holding up my
ticket. She looked and laughed and held up
hers.

"Same flight. Looks like you were
right."

"Right about?" I asked. The cashier
called out my order number as I went to get
the food. I also got an equally big bag of
Polynesian sauce because who knew if I
would find it where I was going.

"You were right about your life. This
is pretty romantic comedy-ish, same flight
back to New York." She laughed, waiting for
me to respond, but I didn't. She continued
before the pause grew too awkward. "Are
your parents coming?"

"No. It's just a connection for me."
"Where you headed?"
"I'm not sure." We stood and shared

301

food like we always had. I had a sandwich
in one hand and in the other balanced the
sauce on our drink. She held the fries for
us to eat from in one hand and her sandwich
in the other. The occasional shuffle back
and forth for the napkin out of the bag.

We laughed as she wiped my face. We
hadn't missed a step in what we used to be.
"So, what did you mean when you said you
didn't miss the party?" I continued.

"I was there for most of the funeral,
right until it was just you and the guys
all there. And then I left."

"Of course. They knew you were there.
I'm gonna kill them."

"No. I only told Hill when I was in
town the day of the funeral, and she said
she wouldn't say anything, so I doubt
anyone else knew." She went to say more
before the gate agent made an announcement
to start the boarding. We backed away while
people slowly swarmed in, waiting for their
group number to be called.

"Hillary said you got some big
opportunity," she went on. "Am I going to
be watching your work on the big screen
soon?"

"Just a YouTube screen at first," I
laughed, "after that, then who knows."

"I'm sure she's proud of you. You know
that, right, Caleb?" she said, turning to
look at me. "I know that I damn sure am."

"Thank you." The gate agent called for

group five, which was Brooklyn's group, but she didn't budge. I'm glad she didn't.

"I should have paid my respects properly, not just from feet away behind a tre—"

"No, I get it."

"It's just I wrote you and never heard bac—"

"I didn't know what to say."

"You always knew what to say."

"Yeah, but you thought I didn't mean it. Or that none of it was real," I said, feeling the weight slide off my shoulders. "You know what was real? Realizing that I was right and that every love story ends in tragedy if you wait long enough. I should have just stuck to what I believe. If I hadn't let you talk me into thi— No, if I would have just stuck to my ideals…" I trailed off, catching myself rambling.

"Then maybe neither of us would be here right now," she said, grabbing my hand.

"No. I know that it's just, maybe we would still be friends."

"Maybe we were going to fall for each other eventually. We couldn't have just stayed friends."

"Maybe." I laughed. "Reminds me of something Grams said to me."

"Life went so fast when we were together, but in a good way. I find myself asking how I, rather, we, ended up here.

It's like we both drove and we just allowed it."

Brooklyn's words hypnotized me. I used her words as colors and moved it around a canvas to help paint a picture. I pictured me driving on a sunny day down a long desert road, music blaring. I downshift to pick up speed, when all of a sudden, Brooklyn appears in the passenger seat. The music is gone now. All I can hear is the hum of the engine and her singing the lyrics to whatever song was playing before.

I upshift to go even faster. The speed increases as she grabs the steering wheel. She slides her feet out of her shoes and into my lap. It's night now, the headlights, moon, and stars are the only lights.

She slowly lifts herself up and slides into my lap and puts her feet on the pedals. I slide out from behind her into the passenger seat. The pavement is gone now, and signs blur by as Brooklyn downshifts to go even faster, making the car howl. The signs read dead end ahead, but neither of us cares. I place my hand on hers as we shift again together.

A wall in the distance crawls closer and closer to us.

And like a dream, I wake up when Brooklyn says, "You were right," bringing me back into the conversation.

"I wish I wasn't."

"No, I'm glad you were. I was right too. You helped me see love isn't just the good things, it's the everything. But it's definitely not just the bad either."

"You and Grams both helped me see that." I smiled at her. The gate agent's death glare caught my eye, and I saw everybody around us had boarded already. We ran over to get scanned in, then walked down the jet bridge and stopped right before the plane.

"Was it worth it?" she asked. I laughed. Before I could respond, she put her finger over my lips. "Think about it?" she continued, squeezing my hands. "Let me know after the flight?"

I nodded and agreed as we walked onto the plane. Our seats weren't near each other, which I thought was a good thing. But at the same time, I wished they were.

Before the flight attendant started her safety routine, I took the cookie out and contemplated. It made me think of the first time we baked weed brownies with Grams. As the thought of me not wanting this cookie anymore—no matter who had baked it—crossed my mind, the man in the row behind me nudged my seat, making me fumble and drop the cookie.

'Thanks, Grams,' I thought.

I slept, dreaming a montage of me and Brooklyn. How her smile made me feel when I was the one causing it, versus not seeing it at all, to seeing it today. The comforting warmth from it, the numbing cold without it, the refreshing nostalgia of it.

Landing woke me. I collected my things and shuffled through the aisle with everyone else racing to get off the plane. Brooklyn was waiting for me outside the gate. We walked in silence for a while, then she took my arm and put it around her shoulders.

"Yes," I said, answering her question before we reached my gate.

"I'm glad." She smiled. "What did you think of the new recipe?" Brooklyn asked.

"I didn't eat it," I confessed.

"I knew you wouldn't" she laughed, "it's not an edible edible, it's a CBD cookie. I don't smoke anymore. It consumed me, but I am still self-medicating, I guess." She laughed again.

"That's great to hear," I said, pulling her in and kissing her on the forehead. That kiss made my heart flutter around like a caged bird, but I didn't let it control me. We walked up to the gate for my next flight, which had already started boarding. Brooklyn took my phone and added a song to my playlist.

"I want you to listen to this when you get over hating me, if you ever do," she said.

"I don't hate you, Brooklyn."

"So you opposite of hate me, then?"

she laughed, wiping a tear from her eye before it had a chance to fall.

I smiled, wishing I had the courage to hug her. I read in her eyes that she was feeling the same way. She put her hand on my chest before she turned and walked away. No goodbyes, I told myself as I watched her leave.

"You amaze me, you know that?" I shouted to her. I felt like I could see her smile spread from ear to ear.

She spun around and shouted back, "Stay away from mazes, Clark Kent. They are just riddled with dead ends."

I watched her wipe her cheek as she turned around, disappearing in the traffic of people. I grabbed my bag and got in line to have my boarding pass scanned.

When I walked through the doors of the jet bridge, I exited into the corner office of Director Griselda Finch. The corner office had been the foreman's office, and it faced inward to the warehouse where filming was always being done. She stood in the glass above us day in and day out, haunting the sets with her presence.

I knocked on the open door and she turned as if to tear me a new asshole, but didn't when she saw it was me. She snatched my manuscript and pointed for me to sit down. I sat in a chair in front of a woman that looked like she hadn't smiled in days.

She flipped through my script page by page, so fast I was sure she couldn't have read more than one line on each.

"It's rubbish, honestly," she said.

"Oh, okay," I replied, standing immediately.

"No, sit down." She fanned the pages at me. "It's fine, really, the writing, I mean. It's his life that's rubbish… proper funny…" Griselda spoke with a lot of pauses in between each of her phrases, making it hard for anyone to know if she was done with her thought, gearing up to shit all over it, or actually considering whatever topic was brought to her. "I mean honestly… it's just… not…" She trailed off finally, using her hands to finish what she was trying to say.

"It's unbelievable?" I tried to guide her.

"It's not believable! I mean, dating a girl who he only sees at work, her getting engaged to her actual boyfriend."

"Yeah, but—"

She waved my manuscript at me to cut me off before I could finish defending myself. She flipped back through the pages to make her point.

"The job hosting an engagement party for her, the poor mate not knowing what the party is for… its bennin' stuff, like funny."

That's another thing she liked to do,

explain her quirky English slang terms to me in a sort of degrading 'silly boy' tone. Before I could speak and try to defend myself again, she continued, "It's just a shit life the mate lives, yeah? Unlucky… but we need more than… misfortune… we need…" She threw down the papers and started using her hands again.

I reached across the table, picking up my manuscript.

"DARK!" she finally screamed.

"Make it… darker?" I unintentionally mocked her.

"Or don't, Casey." She shrugged.

"Caleb."

"Caleb. Right. Just stick to ad ideas for now. You know, what we pay you for."

I stood up and walked out of her office down the rusty stairs. Sara was walking up with a paper in her hands, as if to present something next. We flashed each other a false look of good luck, being we were each other's competition.

A week after starting this job, turns out the studio ran into some money issues. I knew we were going to be relocating, but never to a place like this. I got to see London for the three days I was there and slept in the back room of production storage on a prop bed.

Now we live in a city called Douglas on the Isle of Man. I'm not sure if it's a part of the UK or a part of Ireland, and neither are most of the people here. We focus on whoring ourselves out for commercials to keep the lights on until Griselda thinks we have the perfect show. I've been here a little over two months, and it's definitely been a big adjustment.

The goal of the company is to shoot a pilot or two of a show, move back to London, and go from there. Besides me, there are four other writers that work on set, and we are all pitching show ideas every chance we get between commercials.

Them, they keep coming up with shows and pilots. Me, I keep tweaking what I've been writing for the past year or so, which gives me more free time to do commercial ideas. This also makes Griselda actual money and me kind of the less hated out of the five.

I thought about using my return ticket to go back home and start over. Only thing stopping me was not knowing which home to go to. That sure would be darker for my character, giving up.

That thought was the one I needed. I ran back up the stairs to Griselda's office. I bust through the door to the boss laying across her desk and my colleague (a.k.a. writing competition) falling away from the desk and stumbling over a chair. Griselda sat up on her elbows with an annoyed expression on her face and crossed her legs. She picked up and began to flip

310

through whatever manuscript Sara had brought her while Sara refused to face me as she touched up her makeup in a pocket mirror.

That is when I put two and two together. "Ummm, I can come back later," I said, inching my way out of the thick tension that filled the office.

"Casey, if you leave this room you are fired," Griselda threatened casually, not missing a beat as she continued flipping through the pages. I sat quietly and looked up at the ceiling, counting the number of tiles. I could now feel death stares from Sara, which confirmed my suspicions of what the hell I had almost walked in on. If only AJ was here. He would have tried to join in, I'm sure of it.

I reached for my phone to text him, but just then Griselda rolled up the paper and handed it to Sara like a bone to a dog.

"S-so what do you think?" Sara stuttered.

"It was… better last time… but we were interrupted now, weren't we?" I did everything in my power not to bust out laughing hearing this.

"I meant the scr-"

"Hush. I know what you meant. No one cares about vampires."

"You said make it darker. Vampires are darker."

"I can just come back," I pleaded,

while slowly standing.

"Caleb, you think I like repeating myself, yeah?"

"No, ma'am."

"Why are you here? New commercial idea for the reversible tampons?"

"Not yet. It's about the show I was just in here about."

"Sara, sit down and take notes. He's the best writer we have here, besides me."

"Can I freshen up a bit first?" Sara asked, picking up her papers from off the desk.

"No," Griselda said before turning her attention to me.

"Well, you said darker, so I was thinking what if the guy is planning to kill himself every time something unfortunate happens to him, but then like something comes up so he just puts it off for later."

"On with it then," she said. I think it was an interested tone, but I'm not sure. I plowed ahead anyway.

"Like his girlfriend breaks up with him, so he decides to kill himself, but then his grandma gets sick. So he goes to take care of her."

Griselda walked around the room, thinking on the idea. I looked at my phone and saw a text from Sara, who was sitting beside me: "Does she make you give h-"

I stopped reading immediately, since I

knew where the text was going to go, and
pretended to not read her message at all.

"Maybe eventually the grandma dies…
and he's gonna kill himself… but…" Griselda
started talking with her hands again.

"But he gets a cat," I answered.

"Yes! Brilliant! Okay, Caleb, write it
up and I will see if I can find some money
in the budget! Now the both of you, piss
off so I can get a proper rest."

I walked out of the office as fast as
I could, but Sara pulled me by the back of
my shirt collar. She walked with me down
the stairs and then pushed me into a
corner.

"Well?"

"Well what?"

"What do you think of what just
happened in there?" she stated more than
asked.

I didn't know how to play my next
words. I think Sara had something against
me. One day during our lunch break,
Griselda walked in the breakroom and I
asked for some of her popcorn and she gave
me the rest of her bag. I was teased by
everyone for it, being called a kiss ass or
pet, but for Sara, she saw it as some sort
of challenge.

"Vampires do suc-"

"You think everything's a joke, innit?

"I mean, if it's funny." I tried to
lighten the mood.

"You are proper insane, yeah? How do you do it?"

"What?"

"Be so casual with a blooming heartless monster like her."

I laughed. "She's not a monster. And if she is, monsters have hearts. I'm familiar with the type." I smiled again.

She grabbed me by my shirt, not seeing what I thought was so funny. Sara had arrived a day after me, announcing she was desperate and would do anything to stay ahead, which is why I think she had such a hard time.

People on set of the shampoo commercial were staring at the scene she was causing, and Sara laughed after realizing there was now an audience, trying to play off her 'wobbly.' I'd heard a guy at a market use that word to describe his kid's tantrum, and thought it was the best adjective for this moment.

She stormed off, but I called out to her before she got too far. "Hey!"

She turned around to look at me.

"Still Italian tonight with the production crew?" I asked.

"Yeah. I think Duncan is gonna drive me if you want a ride later."

"Sounds great."

"Nineteen hundred, yeah?" she asked.

I gave her a thumbs-up as she turned and walked away again. I laughed at myself, thinking how these types of women always make their way into my life.

I smiled as I walked to the back of the building and then outside to the alleyway. I saw the same cat that's been meowing for days outside my apartment. It likes to hang out around the freezer of the restaurant across the small cobblestone way. I had made myself a makeshift studio apartment in the basement of the warehouse, so I guess it and I were neighbors.

I went downstairs and grabbed a can of tuna out of the plastic bag on my couch. I popped the top and went back upstairs to lure the cat in. She followed me, so I put the food on my improvised coffee table made of storage containers.

She jumped up, sending orange fur flying everywhere. I walked into the bathroom to open the only window in the apartment and then back to the couch. I reached in that same bag and pulled out a flea collar and popped two Benadryl. As soon as the cat was done eating, it went and lay on top of my miniature fridge in the corner.

I opened my laptop to make the necessary edits to my script. The cat jumped down from its perch and rubbed itself against my legs, I assumed as a thank you. I picked it up to get a good look at her, as she didn't take her eyes off my refrigerator. She was either super greedy or had some weird attraction to fridges.

I laughed as a thought crossed my mind, and before I could dismiss it, the cat looked at me and began to growl. I dropped her onto the floor, but she jumped into my lap, spun around and made herself comfortable. I carefully put the flea collar around her neck as she purred loudly and contently.

My eyes watered. I assumed from allegories… at least that's what I told myself.

Life is a story. History, her-story, it all has a beginning, middle. And even if we don't know when it's coming, it has an end. I still think we should try harder to remember that at some point, we will be a main character in someone else's story too. We'll play a role in somebody else's movie, help turn the page in someone else's book, be the reason for the emotion hitting so hard in a stanza of a poem.

No matter what metaphor you use, it's true, you just can't help it. You can't control the genre, the narrative, and you probably won't be able to see the final product. You won't even know the impact you will have in most people's lives or the impact their life will have on you. Or maybe you will.

I still think we don't control our own

stories, not entirely. Yes, we are constantly living out the choices, decisions, and mistakes of a younger and dumber us. Whether that be six months, two years, or an hour ago, it's still us.

Most of the time, things turn out great. Sometimes there's that one thing that happens that pops up and makes us feel like our whole lives are derailed. When that happens, we harp on it and dwell on it and relive it; but why, if we aren't going to learn from it?

My grandma used to say the past is a foreign world to learn from and that we should be students of it instead of just tourists to it. We visit with pictures, videos, and memories, escaping to enjoy those good times. What conversation made you laugh in that one picture that gave you that horrible face and posture? Trying to remember how much better your drunken Jessica Simpson karaoke set with the guys sounded in person versus in that video. Maybe rubbing the envelope of an old letter, taking a deep inhale and trying to catch faint notes of the perfume it was drenched in when it was handed to you.

The present world is steered by a younger you. A younger, dumber, naiver, maybe happier version of you. Sometimes, I have to stop being who I am and try to remember who I might be.

All those decisions were made for a

reason. We have to learn from the past, not avoid it, or we will just keep reliving the same story over and over. At some point, you'll end up in one of those roles in somebody else's story.

As long as you are learning from mistakes, you will be prepared for the plot twists. Or maybe you won't.

I've learned not to try to avoid falling in love. It's going to happen. Could be temporarily, or at the wrong time. Maybe it will be forever or even too late, but in the end, it will all be worth it.

Gabriel **K**ristopher **Keaton**. Born in
Brooklyn, New York, raised in the
Lunenburg County, Virginia. G is a
storyteller of many mediums who will try
almost anything once. He's a creator of
worlds, bender of realities, butt of his
own jokes, and recovering procrastinator.
Dead End Thrills is Gabriel's first
published work to the masses, but it will
not be his last.

Made in the USA
Lexington, KY
04 November 2019